Finders Keepers

Finders Keepers

by Andrea Spalding

BEACH HOLME PUBLISHING LIMITED
Victoria, B.C.

This edition is published by Beach Holme Publishers, 4252 Com-merce Circle, Victoria, B.C., V8Z 4M2 with the assistance of The Canada Council and the B.C. Ministry of Tourism and Culture.

Cover Art and Interior Illustrations: © 1995 by Gillian Hughes
Cover Design: Barbara Munzar
Production Editor: Antonia Banyard
Printed and Bound in Canada by Webcom

Canadian Cataloguing in Publication Data

Spalding, Andrea.
    Finders keepers

ISBN 0-88878-359-0

    I. Title.
PS8587.P213F56 1995   jC813'.54   C95-910668-5
PZ7.S62Fi 1995

Dedicated to Joe Crowshoe
and the people of the Peigan Nation
in southern Alberta

In this time of unrest and distress over land rights, equal justice and equal rights, the Peigan people have chosen to stretch out their hands to other Canadians and share some aspects of their culture to promote understanding. This decision was not an easy one to make.

Finders Keepers is the direct result of a sharing at Head-Smashed-In Buffalo Jump. It was a gift that has enriched my life.

I have tried to use this gift with respect and to pass it on in a different form to help another group of people engaged in a long struggle, children with learning disabilities.

In my childhood I learned an old folk rhyme:

Finders, keepers
Losers, weepers

May we all find outstretched hands and become "keepers."

Andrea Apalding
Pender Island, B.C.

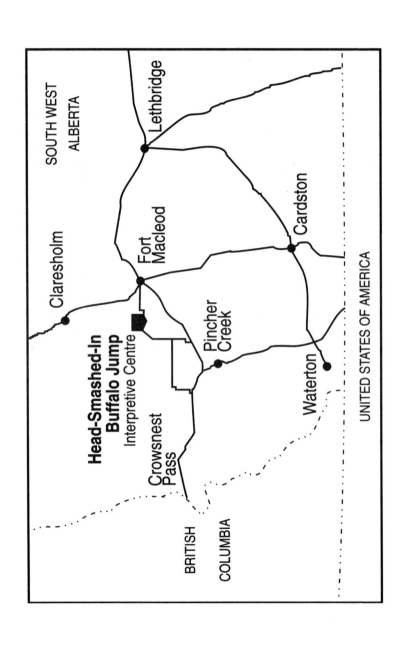

SOUTH WEST
ALBERTA

Lethbridge

Claresholm

Fort
Macleod

Cardston

Head-Smashed-In
Buffalo Jump
Interpretive Centre

Pincher
Creek

Crowsnest
Pass

Waterton

BRITISH
COLUMBIA

UNITED STATES OF AMERICA

Introduction

This book is a work of fiction. While Fort Macleod, Fort Macleod Museum, and Head-Smashed-In Buffalo Jump are real places, I have taken artistic licence with their proximity to each other and the interlinking topography. All the characters in the story are figments of my imagination, so are the plots and situations. Any resemblance to real people is purely coincidental.

Though the museum aspects of the plot are fictitious, the issues dealt with reflect current concerns of Canadians. I wish that learning disabilities were a figment of my imagination. Unfortunately, they are a very real handicap, and children exhibiting some combination of the difficulties described can be found in almost every classroom. There are also many other learning disabilities not described, so please do not attempt diagnosis from this book. Go to a qualified professional or ask for information from the Learning Disabilities Association of Canada.

FINDERS

Chapter One

Danny ran unsteadily across the prairie pasture towards the irrigation ditch on the far side. He threw himself among the tall grasses and shrubs edging the ditch and buried his face in his arms. His chest heaved, not just with exertion, but with the aftermath of dry sobs.

"I can't believe I've done it—run away from school," he gasped out loud. "Now I'm really in for it." He wriggled deeper into the safety of the concealing grass but he was so scared that his body shook and the grasses quivered and rustled in response.

Above him, the noon sun blazed, a newly polished spring sun that melted the remnants of winter and promised warm days ahead. It comforted Danny and his body relaxed slightly into the earth. But when a meadowlark dripped its honeyed notes into the air, Danny angrily stuffed his fingers in his ears. He didn't want anything interrupting him. He needed to figure things out. He lay still for a long time.

A sharp jab roused him.

"Hey. You dead or somethin'?"

Danny rolled over and squinted at another boy's dark head silhouetted between him and the sun.

The boy moved back with a tiny sigh of relief. "You had me scared."

Danny swiftly dragged his sleeve across his face, sat up cautiously and glanced behind. The town of Fort Macleod looked as usual, pretty quiet. No sign of an irate teacher chasing over the fields after him. But he slid his bum down the steep slope of the irrigation ditch towards the water's edge, putting the concealing earth bank between him and the town. The other boy followed.

Danny looked sideways with interest. Fort Macleod was a small town and he knew practically everyone living there. But this kid with his black hair and dark eyes was from the reserve. Danny had seen him around the stores, but he didn't know him. He was about Danny's age and Danny wondered why he was wandering around the fields on his own.

"How come you're not in school?" Danny blurted out.

The boy grinned, picked a up a stone and threw it expertly across the dull water below. Both boys watched admiringly as it skipped seven times before disappearing into the depths.

"Teacher quit," he replied laconically. "We don't get another till Monday."

"WOW!" Danny gasped in admiration. A wonderful new world opened up before him. A world in which teachers quit and you couldn't find a replacement. A hundred scenarios raced through his brain. What if Mr. Berg quit? No more yelling, no more DTs. No more dreading being chosen to spell out loud. No-one sniggering when he stumbled over his tables. No more being called stupid when he couldn't do written work.

"So. Why aren't you in school?" The boy interrupted his daydream.

Danny thought for a minute. Suddenly the world that had seemed so desperate held new hope. With the trace of a grin on his lips, he turned to the unknown boy. "I quit," he said firmly.

There was a moment's silence, then the boy gave a

chuckle and slapped Danny on the back. That did it. Danny's precarious balance gave way and he slithered down the slippery grass-covered slope towards the cold grey water.

"Help!" Danny grabbed the boy's arm. Down they both slithered, stopping only on the very edge of the bank, Danny with one foot in the water.

"Geez, that's cold." Danny ripped off his sneaker and wobbled on one leg while wringing out his sock. Then he hopped around shaking the sock and shoe in the air, trying to figure if the sun was hot enough to dry them.

The boy laughed. Danny looked at him and then down at his dripping shoe and sock and realized he was showering the boy; he grinned and again flicked the wet sock in his direction. The boy ducked and scooped up a handful of water and flung it over Danny. Danny retaliated and in seconds both boys were soaked, laughing, and breathless.

"What's your name?" panted Danny as they lay on their backs and figured out what to do next.

"Joshua Brokenhorn," replied the boy. "What's yours?"

"Danny Budzynski. My dad runs the general store in Fort Macleod, and we live in the white farmhouse on the highway just west of town."

Joshua nodded. "Walked past it today." He punched Danny on the arm. "Your dog barked at me."

"Aw. He barks at everyone, but he wags his tail at the same time. He's a dumb mutt," added Danny quickly so that Joshua wouldn't think he was nuts over his dog.

Joshua lay back and chewed on a grass stalk. Danny looked curiously at him. He'd never really talked to a kid from the reserve before, and he'd never visited the reserve. He'd heard stories. Some of the grownups in town didn't seem to like Indians, but Danny thought they were neat; in fact he admired them and sometimes he wished he was one. Not a modern Indian, but a warrior of the plains who never went to school, but hunted buffalo and lived in a teepee. Sometimes Danny would pay his quarter to go inside the museum in Fort Macleod. He'd wander around looking at the Indian beadwork, the collection of arrowheads and the old photos, (especially the ones showing the Sun Dance, with the warrior pulling against the sinews threaded through his chest) and he'd imagine what life would be like as an Indian.

"What's it like on the reserve?" he asked hesitantly.

Joshua looked solemn. "Oh, we scalp white folk and sit around drumming and waiting for the buffalo to come."

Danny's eyes widened. "You joking?"

Joshua laughed. "'Course I am. What do you think it's like?"

Danny shook his head. "Dunno. You're the first reserve kid I've talked to."

"Well, Danny Bud-whatever-it-is, you're the first Ukrainian kid I've talked to. What's it like at your place?"

"Aw, we just sit around and eat perogies," Danny offered with a grin.

"Hey, you're OK." Joshua stretched and got to his feet. "Want to come and see the eagles?"

Danny cautiously climbed to the top of the bank and looked over. Everything was still quiet. "What the heck. I'm in big trouble anyway." And he slid back down.

The two boys headed along the ditch swiping last year's grasses with their hands as they passed, seeing who could send the dead seed heads flying farthest.

"Where do the Eagles play? They've never played the Macleod Cougars."

"Not a hockey team... Eagles... Real birds."

"Oh, birds." Danny's tone echoed his disappointment. His vision of a stolen afternoon watching a hockey game was rudely shattered. "What do we want to go and see birds for?"

Joshua turned and patiently explained. "No, not just birds. Bald Eagles. Lots of them." His voice rose excitedly. "They fly along this side of the Rockies on their spring migration. They're going to the lakes up north."

Danny was unconvinced. "I've seen eagles," he said. "They circle above our farm sometimes."

6

"Those are Golden Eagles," Joshua explained. "But these are the Bald Eagles. You see them in southern Alberta only at this time of the year. They're special. My grandfather told me they'd be here for the next few days. I promised to meet him on his lookout hill. Come on."

Joshua scrambled up the side of the ditch and headed west across the farmlands. Danny followed, not sure that eagles were really interesting, but Joshua seemed OK. Besides, it would fill in the time until school finished and he could go home.

Chapter Two

The boys jogged across endless fields and tracks and slithered under a barbed wire fence with a faded NO TRES-PASSING sign. Danny stopped. "Hey, is this reserve land? Am I trespassing?" he asked uncomfortably.

Joshua barely lessened his long easy stride. "You're with me, aren't you?" he tossed over his shoulder.

"Guess so." Danny ran to catch up and they continued together for another half kilometre.

"How much longer?" panted Danny. "Where is this lookout place anyway?"

Joshua stopped and pointed. The land rose and fell ahead of them in ever increasing waves. In the far distance the sun gleamed on the Rocky Mountains, a jagged white capped wall edging Danny's world. The mountains were constant reminders of another world, one beyond the prairies. They beckoned.

"The mountains!" Danny sputtered. "They're miles away."

Joshua shook his head. "Nah! The next rise." He pointed again. "See, there's Naaahsa, my grandfather."

Danny squinted for a better look. The top of the next rise was still far away, but he could see it clearly. He couldn't see anyone on it though. Joshua continued to point so Danny scanned it again carefully. He shook his head. "The only thing up there is that old tree stump."

Joshua grinned and started up the rise. "Better not let grandfather hear you call him that," he tossed over his shoulder. "He might think it's disrespectful."

Puzzled, Danny stared at Joshua's back, then his eyes raked the hilltop again. The tree stump could be a person. A person sitting on the ground. But why would Joshua's Grandfather be sitting on the ground in the middle of a field? He headed up to find out.

At the crest of the hill Danny stopped, feeling uncomfortable. An old man was sitting cross-legged on a blanket, another folded neatly across his lap. His iron-grey hair was parted in the middle and woven into two long braids that hung down over his chest and ended in bright red elastics. He sat there still and silent, his hands in his lap, gazing across the field. His face reminded Danny of the museum photos of long dead chiefs. Stern, strong and unreadable, and definitely different. Danny was the odd person out here. He felt awkward, a little frightened and unsure of what he had got himself into.

Joshua settled cross-legged, slightly behind the old man. Danny scuffed his feet nervously. "Er, hi," he ventured, darting a look at the old man's face.

The old man's eyes briefly met Danny's. He gave a tiny nod then returned to gazing at the field. His lips moved silently as though he was talking to himself.

Joshua laid his fingers on his lips, patted a space on the blanket, and motioned Danny to join him. Danny tiptoed over and sat down. "What's he doing?" he mouthed to Joshua.

"Praying," Joshua mouthed back.

Danny felt even more uncomfortable and wished he'd not asked. Wasn't praying something people did privately? Or at mass? It wasn't something you did in the middle of a field, especially when other people were around. He shifted his legs uneasily and looked at the sky, the landscape, the ground. Anywhere except at the old man.

They sat for a long time.

Gradually a change came over Danny. Instead of feeling uncomfortable and looking around desperately for something to grab his attention, he began to really look. To see and absorb the tiny details of the landscape.

It was an ordinary scene. The sort he saw every day, had seen a hundred times before but never really looked at. He was sitting in the middle of a field, the ploughed ridges sharp beneath his buttocks. Ice crystals sparkled in the hollows despite the strength of the sun. Before him, the swirled chocolate ground rolled away into a wide shallow valley. It stopped abruptly as a road slashed through a string of shallow sloughs, their edges hazing with the spring greening. Beyond, the rangeland swelled upwards in a ripple of bleached gold grass, towards the hovering mountains. Behind and on either side of him the ground fell away, dissolving into a view of patchwork prairie that expanded endlessly onward, dominated only by the massive spread of blue sky.

Danny shrank deep into his jacket, feeling tiny and insignificant. He closed his eyes. That was when he noticed the wind.

The wind curled around him, lifting the hair off his forehead. It whispered insistently in his ears and wafted under his nose. Suddenly Danny felt in contact with his world again. He grinned as he recognized the pungent whiff of pigs and cattle from Mr. MacVey's farm on the next quarter section. He identified the distant throb of a tractor, and the tiny peep of a young gopher. He took a deep breath and filled his lungs with the clean fragrance of wild sage and the full-bodied smell of living, breathing earth. With eyes still closed Danny stretched his arm out and felt for the edge of the blanket. He stretched a little further and dug his fingers into the surface of the soil. The ground was too hard for him to be able to do more than pick up a piece of the crusted surface. His hand closed around it and crumbled it to dust. The heat of his palm released more of its rich earthy aroma. Danny opened his eyes and lifted his fist into the air. He spread his fingers and watched the wind lift the soil grains and swirl them across the field.

About 30 metres away, a small patch of white stirred.

A tingle ran down Danny's spine. He froze, hardly daring to breathe. He was looking right into the fierce eyes of an adult Bald Eagle.

The bird was hunched on the ground, resting. Its black feathers blended into the dark ridges of earth. Even the bold white head melted into the background. It could have been a patch of ice, or a piece of garbage caught in the furrow. If the bird hadn't turned sharply to see if Danny's movement was a threat, Danny would never have spotted it.

Bird and boy gazed unblinkingly at each other.

"You have the gift to see." The old man's voice was a whisper, soft, almost part of the landscape. "When you become at one with the earth, then you are able to see clearly."

Danny wasn't sure whether he really heard the words being spoken, or if they'd somehow 'appeared' in his head. All he knew was that he was seeing in a way he had never seen before.

He concentrated his whole being on the eagle.

Danny accepted the fierceness of the bird's gaze and silently told it he meant no harm. How could a boy ever threaten such a bird, after seeing the sharpness of its hooked yellow beak, the strength and speed of the folded wings, the grasp of its hooked talons, and its incredible single-mindedness to survive?

The eagle acknowledged its dominance by drawing itself up and unhunching its shoulders. Six feet of wings slowly unfurled and leisurely stretched. Then, instead of the bird soaring upward, it was as though it paused in the air, relaxed its talons and let the ground drop away beneath it.

Three sets of eyes wonderingly followed the spiralling upward flight. Then a cry from behind made them jump. A second Bald Eagle swooped over them and gave chase.

Spiralling rapidly, it climbed higher and higher until level with the first bird. For a long moment the two eagles were tiny black specks circling each other. Then they leaped towards each other with talons outstretched, and became one.

Danny's mouth opened in a silent gasp.

Locked together as if in mortal combat, the eagles tumbled earthward in ever increasing momentum. There was a powerful rush of displaced air and the two bodies flashed past Danny, separating only an inch or two from the ground before gliding off in opposite directions.

A single tail feather floating gently earthwards was all that remained of the tempestuous display. Danny eagerly reached out to grab it, but it wafted beyond his fingers to land at the feet of the old man.

The old man leaned forward and gently ran his fingers over the feather's length. Then he picked it up and looked from it to Danny. "Young men have to earn eagle feathers," he said gently. "Your time will come," and he carefully stowed it inside his jacket.

Suddenly Danny felt angry. It wasn't fair! The eagle feather was his. He was the one the eagle looked at. Frustrated, he scrambled to his feet. His sudden movement caused a ripple of disturbance across the field. He paused uncertainly, and looked around. Several patches of white stirred, then five, ten, no... at least twenty Bald Eagles spread their wings and one by one soared upwards. He had been sitting in a field among twenty Bald Eagles, and never noticed.

No wonder the old Indian had watched for so long. No wonder Joshua was so quiet. They must both think he was real mean scaring the birds like that. "I'm sorry," stammered Danny. "I, I didn't realize. I only saw the one eagle. I didn't see the others."

"When you are at one with the earth, then you will see clearly," the old man said.

"Well, er yes. I've gotta go. See ya some time, Joshua," and Danny took to his heels in embarrassment and ran.

When he reached the far pasture he looked back. Joshua and his grandfather were silhouetted against the sky, carefully folding up the blankets. Danny scanned the blue above them with a heavy heart. There was not an eagle to be seen. Then he saw Joshua pause before disappearing over the ridge, and look in Danny's direction. Danny looked hopefully back. Joshua raised his hand in farewell.

Heartened, Danny raised his in reply, turned towards home and slipped and fell flat on his back

He sat up and examined his runners. His right foot had skidded on a fresh cow pie. "Gross," he muttered crossly as he looked around for something to scrape off the muck. He spotted a stick half buried in the ground and scraped around it until he could pull it out. The end was stuck so he gave it a sharp tug. A shower of dirt and stones came with it. One stone caught his eye. Danny picked it up, and gently turned it over and over in his fingers. It wasn't a stone, it was a delicately shaped stone point. He whipped his head around.

"Hey JOSHUA!" he yelled excitedly, but the ridge behind him was empty. He shrugged, no big deal. They had taken the eagle feather home. He'd take this, a genuine arrowhead, an unbroken one too! He slipped it carefully into his back pocket, cleaned up his shoe and headed home to the farm.

Chapter Three

Meeting Joshua and his grandfather had distracted Danny completely from his worries, but as he approached his farm driveway, the fear of getting into big trouble slowed his steps. His hand shook as he opened the gate and tried to figure out how he was going to explain "playing hookey" to his mom.

His dog bounded up to meet him, tail and ears waving.

"Down Ringo!" Danny commanded gruffly. "I can't play now."

Ringo barked and continued to eagerly circle Danny, mouthing his hand and racing off to retrieve and drop a favourite stick. Danny ignored him. Ringo whined in protest and sank onto his haunches.

The kitchen door flew open framing Danny's mother, stern and tense. "Where do you think you've been?" she asked. But before Danny could answer she reached out and pulled him inside. "You go straight to your room young man. I've got to phone the Mounties, the school and your dad, and tell them you're back."

Danny found his voice. "The Mounties?" he squeaked.

"Yes, the Mounties," repeated his mother angrily. "Who

else do you call when a ten-year-old kid disappears from school and is missing all afternoon?"

Danny felt sick. The emotions of the day suddenly became too much for him. He looked up at his mother, the blood draining from his face. She stared back, then her face softened.

"Oh Danny," she said, bending down and hugging him hard. "I was so worried." She brushed the hair off his forehead. "Are you OK?"

Danny nodded and hugged her abruptly. "I didn't mean to scare you... I was safe... I was only in the fields." Then he pulled back and looked at her with a stubborn expression on his face. "But I'm never going back to school again. EVER!" And he ran to his bedroom and slammed the door.

Danny lay stiffly on his bed. He knew he was in deep trouble. But how could he be in the wrong and yet feel so right? School was the pits. It wasn't just him that was wrong, Mr. Berg was awful. But who was going to believe him?

Danny tried to organize his thoughts so he could explain his desperation to his parents. It was a repeat of his last report card when Mr. Berg had said he was lazy and didn't try and his dad believed Mr. Berg! It wasn't fair. No matter how hard Danny tried, school was a disaster. Words in the textbooks wouldn't stay still on the pages. He found it hard to understand the explanations. As for numbers, they were like bits of spaghetti, always slipping out of his grasp. Then there was gym. In gym he always got mixed up with right and left and fell over and everyone laughed at him and called him dumb. When people laughed, or someone yelled at him, then his brain would stop working.

Danny thought it all through very carefully. He wished he could explain school to his dad. His dad had found school easy. His dad wanted Danny to do well, go to business college, then take over the store. Danny hated helping in the store. He made mistakes. Then his dad yelled.

Danny sighed. "Oh well, maybe my parents will discover I've got a brain tumor or something, and I'll never have to go back to school, or work in the store, or anything."

Danny lay back on his pillow and imagined the scene.

"Danny Budzynski is seriously ill," announced the princi-pal in assembly. "In fact, he is not expected to live long. He has a brain tumor." Everyone at school gasped. Some of the girls start-ed to cry. "I wished we'd been nicer to him," cried his classmates. "Me too," agreed Mr. Berg, who came and begged for forgiveness at his bedside, while Danny, pale and wan, raised his hand and in a frail voice said, "I forgive you all," and died.

There was a sharp rap on the bedroom door. "Supper's ready," called his mother.

Reality was definitely unpleasant. Supper was almost completely silent. "Do you want to talk now or when your dad gets home?" asked his mother stiffly.

Danny poked the chili around his bowl. He'd rather talk to his mom. He knew she'd listen and try to help explain to his father. But that might make things worse. His father was big on him 'being a man' and having 'man to man' talks about problems. "Guess I'll have to talk to dad anyway," he sighed. " But can we do it all together? The once?"

His mother nodded, though she obviously found wait-ing hard. So did Danny. The adventure of a stolen afternoon had completely vanished and he just wanted the day to be over. He dropped his spoon and pushed back his chair. "Can I go mom? I'm not hungry."

"Go where?" asked his mother a shade too quickly.

"To watch TV," answered Danny impatiently. He looked at his mother's anxious eyes. "What's the matter? I'm not an escaped criminal or something." He stomped into the living room, threw himself on the sofa and tried to im-merse himself in a rock video program, but no matter how loud he turned up the music he couldn't stop his ears pick-ing up his mother's jerky movements in the kitchen or stop himself listening for his father's car.

It was a relief when the car did arrive and he heard the slam of the back door, but just as he stood up to join his parents, he heard another voice and his heart dropped to his boots; it was Mr. Hubner, the school principal. Danny sprawled angrily on the sofa again. What was the principal here for? This was Danny's business with his parents. As far as he was concerned, school was history.

His father walked determinedly into the living room, clicked off the TV and stood, straddle-legged in front of it. Mr. Hubner followed and sat down confidently in the easy chair opposite Danny. His mother perched on a straight chair looking uneasy. The small room was suddenly full of large adults.

"Well Danny," boomed Mr. Hubner with a big gummy smile. "I gather you've had a bad day?"

Danny glanced around the room feeling cornered. Three against one. It wasn't fair!

Mr. Hubner leaned forward over his knees, clasped his hands earnestly and dropped his voice. "We're here to help you. When a kid runs away from school it's pretty serious and we need to know why." He stretched out a hand and patted Danny encouragingly on the knee, then leaned back again. "So why don't you take your time and tell us what the problem is?"

Danny felt his brain seize up and his mind go blank. Everything he'd thought of to tell his folks... gone. His brain was in deep-freeze mode. No words, no images, just a big fat zero.

He huddled on the sofa scarcely feeling his body. It was like those zombies in the horror movies. The living dead, that's what he was. No wonder his teacher thought he was dumb.

There was a long and heavy silence.

"Danny," said his father in a warning voice. "Ignoring us isn't going to help. That's just going to get everyone plain mad."

Mad! They were going to get mad. Deep inside Danny felt a small hot spot begin to glow. Well they weren't the only ones who were going to get mad. So was Danny, real mad. A great big M.A.D.

Danny's brain was still locked in deep freeze, so he filled

in his time by staring at Mr. Hubner and waiting for his Adam's apple to bob up and down. Mr. Hubner always did that when he was feeling annoyed but trying to put things in a nice way.

"HRUUMP." Mr. Hubner cleared his throat and his Adam's apple bobbed rapidly. "Er, Danny, when your dad and I were at school, any student who ran away would have got a licking. No questions asked. Right Charlie?"

Danny's dad nodded in agreement.

"Now just a minute!" Danny's mother broke in.

"Let me finish, Jeanie." Mr. Hubner held up a warning hand. "I know, times have changed. But if Danny isn't going to cooperate and tell us why he left, then he is going to have to take the consequences and he won't like them."

The threat hung heavily in the air. To Danny's dismay he felt tears of sheer frustration start to gather. Why didn't this guy just leave, then Danny could try talking to his parents. He wished now he'd talked first to his mother. She would listen. Then maybe she'd get his dad to listen. If only the jerky principal would leave.

Mr. Hubner rose heavily to his feet. He seemed to fill the room. "I'm a reasonable man, Danny, so I'm going to give you one more chance. Today's Friday. You think things over this weekend, then be in my office with an explanation at 8:30 am Monday morning."

Danny's hot spot flared up propelling Danny suddenly to his feet. "I'm not going to your office," he yelled. "I'm NEVER going to your office."

"Danny," implored his mother.

"I'm never going to school again." Danny turned and glared at his father. "You can hit me, Dad, or lock me in jail if you like. For nothing you can do to me is as bad as making me go to school." Then he plumped back on the sofa and waited for the sky to fall.

The adults exchanged shocked looks. Mr. Budzynski sighed heavily and shook Mr. Hubner by the hand. "Look, thanks for coming over Al, but I think we better try to get to the bottom of this ourselves. I'll run you back into town."

The Principal nodded and made his way towards the back door. He turned before leaving. "Danny?"

Danny looked up.

"I'm here to help. I'll see you Monday," and the door closed as the two men left.

Danny sat on the sofa, staring at his feet. Now he'd really done it. He'd never answered back to a teacher or principal before. He'd felt like it lots of times. Especially when Mr. Berg was picking on him. But now he'd really done it. He looked across at his mother with big unhappy eyes. "Will dad hit me?"

His mother came and sat beside him and pulled him close. "Has your dad ever hit you?" Danny shook his head. "Well he's not going to start now. It's just it's been a worry for all of us and when people are worried they get cross. Mr. Hubner has been as worried as us."

Danny sniffed in disbelief.

"Danny, try and explain. Have you done something really wrong, broken something, hit somebody, even stolen something?" Danny shook his head vigorously.

His mother held him even tighter. "Then has somebody done something to you? Hit you? Touched you? Made you do something you're ashamed to talk about?"

Danny shook his head again and again. His mother looked at him in bewilderment. "Then what is it?"

Danny tried to explain. "It's just school, mom," he explained tiredly. "Not just today, but all the time. It's awful."

His mother continued to hold him close. Danny could feel her trying to choose words and help him. "Lots of kids don't like school Danny, but they don't run away."

"Lots of kids can do the school work. I can't."

His mother sighed. "Oh Danny. We've been through this so many times. You're bright. You can tell me the answers when I ask you questions. What happens?"

Danny shook his head miserably. "Dunno." He looked up at his mother. "Mr. Berg gave us the mental arithmetic test today. Know how many I could do?"

19

His mother shook her head.

"Zilch."

"But you studied for that. You were doing OK as long as you thought about it."

"That's it." Danny thumped the sofa in frustration. "There's no time to think. By the time I could see the question straight in my head, Mr. Berg was on the next one, and the one after that. I didn't even get the first answer down. By then I was too confused."

His mother sighed. "I know. Sometimes math problems get me that way too. But school's not all mental arithmetic. That's only a small part of it."

"Yeah. A big part's this new Social Studies and Language Arts project," said Danny dismally.

"So tell me about that."

"It's this new thing, see, kind of testing us on English and Socials at the same time. Mr. Berg explained it to us this morning. It's awful. We have to choose a subject, research it and write a report on it. The report's got to have illustrations and be at least 10 pages long. We have to do an outline, then a rough copy, then a good copy. The best copy has to have good handwriting and no spelling mistakes and be handed in on time. In six weeks! It will count for 50% of my year's mark in both Social Studies and Language Arts," finished Danny, his voice rising despairingly.

"That doesn't sound too difficult," said his mother slowly. "You've got lots of time. You could do a bit a night. Ten pages sounds a lot but if that includes illustrations it's not bad." She brightened enthusiastically. "You could do something on the Indians you are always researching."

Danny shook his head vehemently and sat on the edge of the sofa. "No Mom. You don't understand. The topic's no problem. I'm interested in lots of stuff. It's the writing and spelling and copying it out. Ten pages... I might as well quit now. I can't do ten pages without any mistakes. I'd have to redo it so many times it would take me ten years. I can't spell, Mom. I can't tell if the words are spelled right or wrong. There's no way I can hand in a report without mistakes." He slumped back into the sofa cushions.

"I... I tried to tell Mr. Berg and he laughed at me and said I was a quitter. Brenda called me a geek and everyone laughed. Even Michael laughed." Danny sniffed. "I'm dead. I might as well quit now. Everyone knows I'm dumb anyway. They all hate me."

"Everyone doesn't hate you Danny, you've got friends, Michael likes you. And I'm sure Mr. Berg doesn't hate you."

Danny's eyes watered. He angrily wiped his sleeve across them. "He hates me the most. Everyone hates me, even Michael. He won't have me on his team in gym 'cause I go the wrong way, or fall over, or drop the ball."

His mother gave him a squeeze and said cheerfully, "So, you play on the other team."

Danny's hurt eyes looked at his mother. "Mom, nobody wants me. Guess you don't know what it's like to be the last one to be chosen all the time."

His mother thought for a long time. "Guess I do, son," she said slowly. "That used to happen to me too."

They hugged silently for a while.

"Tell me about Mr. Berg," said his mother thoughtfully. "Does he yell a lot?" Danny nodded miserably. "What happens to you when he yells?"

Danny shrugged. "I dunno, I get scared I guess. I kind of freeze inside. Like those jack rabbits in the truck headlights at night."

"What happens to your work when you're scared?" she pressed gently.

"That's just it." Danny thumped his knee in frustration. "I can't do it! I know lots of stuff but I can't do it. The words move on the page, or my writing gets all mixed up, letters go the wrong way round and I can't remember how to spell... and..." He gulped. "Everyone laughs when I can't remember my multiplication tables."

His mother reached in her pocket and passed Danny a tissue. He blew his nose noisily. "Mr. Berg says I'm not trying," he continued. "But I am, I really try!" He paused, ashamed. "The kids call me Dummy Danny. I'm just one big Ukrainian joke."

There was a long silence. Eventually Danny pulled away and looked at his mother. She was gazing abstractedly across the room. "You're not listening," he accused.

"Of course I am." She quickly flashed him a smile. "I was thinking." She looked at him searchingly as though she was trying to figure out what to say. "Danny, I believe you. I think there IS a reason for the trouble you're having at school."

Danny's face filled with relief. "Like I've got a brain tumor or something?" he said eagerly.

His mother laughed and ruffled his hair. "No such luck! That's your imagination again, isn't it kid?"

Danny nodded with a sheepish grin.

"I've a friend, Carol." His mother continued. "She's teaching at University and doing some research on how children learn. Some of the things you've told me sound kind of like some of the problems she's researching. Would you mind if I discuss it with her?"

Disinterestedly, Danny shrugged. University stuff wouldn't help him any. "What about Dad?" he asked, "and school?"

"I'll talk to your dad and we'll figure something out. But Danny, you will have to go back to school next week. You know that really, don't you?"

"I guess so," said Danny, shuffling his feet.

"As for friends," continued his mother. "You don't make friends by getting good marks, but by sharing interests and doing things together. If you're no good at a game, try sharing some of your other interests with Mike. Who knows, he might really like some of the things you do."

"I'll think about it," said Danny doubtfully. He yawned, exhausted. "Mom, it's Friday night. Can I watch the movie? It's *Star Trek Meets the Green Slime*."

His mother nodded abstractedly. Danny turned on the TV and settled back on the sofa, his body weak with relief. Thank goodness that was over and it was the weekend. Two whole days without school.

Chapter Four

Danny slept late on Saturday. The events of the previous day had left him physically and mentally exhausted. Tousled and groggy he sat up in bed and tried to catch at the elusive remnants of the dream that had woken him. It was a dream he'd had many times before. The one he'd named 'The Chase'.

In 'The Chase' Danny always found himself running over an endless plain towards a tall tower on the horizon. If he could only reach the tower he'd be safe, but he never could. Panting and gasping, he'd run as hard as he could, and almost be there... and the tower would move. Even as he reached out his hand to touch it, the tower would recede into the distance and he'd have to run faster and further. And all the time something fearful was chasing him. Danny never found out what the fearful thing was, but it was always there, breathing down his neck and filling him with unspeakable panic. He'd wake up just as it reached him.

As usual after the dream, Danny's mouth was dry and bitter, but this time his heart was not racing as hard as it sometimes did, for in this dream there had been something different, something hopeful. His mind gnawed and fretted at the fragmented images floating around his brain. In his dream he'd bent down and picked up something on the plain. Something that filled him with relief, something he could use against the 'thing'.

The images receded and drifted away in the morning sunshine, leaving Danny with a vaguely anxious feeling of loss. He threw back the bedclothes and started to fish around with one foot for some clothes off the floor. He found his Jurassic Park T-shirt and wriggled into his jeans. Feeling a lump in his pocket, he reached in and pulled out the stone point.

It lay in the palm of his hand, gleaming gently in the sunlight. It was beautiful. The friction of his jeans had rubbed and polished the dirt from its surface. It wasn't dull grey rock like some he'd seen in the museum, but chipped from an unusual rock, a cream-colored chert containing faint orange veins. Danny held it up to the light and its edges became almost translucent.

Danny's sense of anxiety vanished. This was what he'd found in his dream, the weapon he could use against the 'thing'. In his sleep his mind had remembered the point. Gently Danny ran his fingertips over the fluted edges. They were thin and sharp. Danny marvelled that they had not been damaged in the years the point had had lain in the ground. "I wonder who made you?" he whispered. "Did an Indian use you to kill a 'thing' chasing him? Maybe you could be my lucky arrow head and protect me?"

Danny carefully wrapped the point in some tissues and returned it to his pocket. It would be nice to know more about it. If he went to the museum he could check it out against the arrowheads on display. He finished dressing, then headed into the kitchen. "Hey Mom," he yelled hopefully. "Any chance of a ride into town?"

Even though Danny rushed through his farm chores and nagged his mother (who seemed to be spending hours on the phone) it was afternoon before they left the house.

"Be back at the store at 5:30 pm," warned Danny's mother as she competently angle-parked in a small space in the

Saturday row of farm trucks on Fort Macleod's main street. "Your Dad and I want to leave right at closing time."

Danny nodded, unlocked his door and slid out of the car.

"Thought you might turn up if I hung around long enough," said a satisfied voice.

Danny looked around.

Joshua was standing in the back of a half-ton, two spaces down. He swung his legs over the tailgate and dropped lightly into the street. "So," he said, "Did you get a licking last night?"

Danny shook his head. "No-oo, but I guess I'll be in trouble on Monday... at school."

Joshua considered. "Naw, you're too quiet. It's the mouthy kids that really get it. You'll just get yelled at."

"Sometimes that's worse than a lickin'." Danny moodily kicked a loose rock chip as visions of Mr. Berg's face, distorted with anger, flashed through his head. "Anyway, I don't want to think about Monday yet. Come on, race you to the museum."

Danny turned and ran up the road, then stopped when he realized Joshua wasn't following. "What's up Joshua? Don't you want to come?" He walked back to where Joshua was standing.

Joshua looked uncomfortable. "This museum. Do you have to pay to get in?"

Danny grinned. "Sure, but it's only a quarter for kids. Do you have any money?" Joshua shook his head.

Danny tipped out his pocket but only found one quarter and two pieces of gum. He passed one of the pieces of gum over. "Here, have this and we'll go find some bottles to take back."

Chewing companionably, Danny and Joshua headed over to the highway and started searching the soggy, matted grass along the ditch.

"Got one." Joshua pounced where the sunlight glinted and triumphantly unearthed a large coke bottle.

"Me too." Danny found two beer bottles in close proximity. A further search uncovered four small pop bottles, three beer cans and a whisky bottle. They sat in the ditch and surveyed their spoils.

"Wow, We're rich!" Joshua took off his jean jacket and wrapped it around the bottles and cans. "That's nearly a dollar's worth. If we can find a few more on the way to the bottle depot we'll have enough for some candies or a slurpee."

He glanced happily at Danny, who was looking at his fingers and counting to himself, a look of intense concentration on his face. When he saw Joshua watching, he stopped and blushed beet red.

"Go on, laugh," said Danny fiercely.

Joshua spread his hands in a gesture of peace. "Hey, man. I'm not laughing. I don't even know what you're doing."

"Figuring."

"Figuring?" repeated Joshua blankly. "Oh, you mean the bottles. That's easy. There's three beer bottles at three cents a bottle, that's nine cents; there's two litre bottles at 20 cents each, that's 49 cents altogether; then there's four pop bottles and two cans at five cents each, that's another 30 cents; that makes 79 cents so far, and if we find..." Joshua trailed off as the flush of embarrassment on Danny's face deepened. "What's up?"

"That!" said Danny sadly. "The figuring out. I can only do it on my fingers."

"OK, so I'll do it. No big deal." Joshua knotted his jacket sleeves together and hoisted the resulting parcel over one shoulder. "My grandfather, he's not too hot at math, and my great grandfather, he couldn't read. It never stopped him being chief though. Come on, let's see if there's more bottles in the back alleys."

Danny scrambled to his feet and they walked back into town, checking out the garbage cans and fence lines. Five more pop cans and a beer bottle were found, then they cashed in their loot at Mrs. Tyler's bottle drop.

Joshua was jubilant as Mrs. Tyler counted out the money. "See. That's $1.09. We keep a quarter for the museum and spend the rest, OK?"

"Don't spend it all at once," said Mrs. Tyler with a deadpan face. The boys looked at her uncomprehendingly.

"No, we'll go to the museum first," Danny replied politely, and was a little startled when she laughed.

The boys raced up the road towards the rebuilt fort. They rounded the corner of the palisade and stopped short. Closed said the notice at the turnstile.

"Oh no!" said Danny in frustration. "I forgot. It's only open in summer."

"Excuse me boys, you're blocking my way." A large woman carrying two buckets and a mop edged past them and opened the gate beside the turnstile.

"Oh, hi Mrs. Saunders," said Danny.

"Might have know it would be you, Danny." She looked across at Joshua. "He practically lived here last summer." She shut the gate. "We're not open yet, Danny. We're only in to organize a new exhibit and spring clean everything for the summer season."

"Please Mrs. Saunders," Danny pleaded. "Can't you let us in? I need to do some research. I really need to look at the arrowheads. Please... we won't damage anything."

"Hmm." Mrs. Saunders surveyed Danny. Joshua had stepped aside to read one of the notices in the wall. "If it was just you I might."

"Joshua won't hurt anything," said Danny eagerly. "He's with me."

Mrs. Saunders looked distrustfully at Joshua's back and leaned towards Danny, dropping her voice. "He's Indian, isn't he?"

Danny looked at her with shocked eyes. "He's my friend," he said quietly.

Mrs. Saunders shrugged and turned to walk away. "No can do," she said. "Come back in May," and she opened the turnstile gate, gave a bump of her hip to close it and disappeared around the building. They heard her footsteps crunching across the gravel in the courtyard.

Angry and embarrassed, Danny muttered "Old Bat," and kicked the gate.

It swung open.

"Quick, we'll show her." Danny grabbed Joshua's arm, pulled him through, and gently closed the gate behind them. "This way."

Chapter Five

Bent double, the two boys fled through the entrance, turned across a small patch of gravel, and dived into a dark doorway. Holding their breath, they flattened themselves against a split log wall and listened—nothing.

Carefully Danny peered back the way they came. There was no one around. He drew in his head and gave the thumbs-up sign.

"Hwee." Joshua let out his breath and relaxed. "That was risky."

"Only when we crossed the gravel. Anyway, she'll never catch us now." Danny grinned cockily. "I know all the hiding places in this fort, and there's lots."

Joshua tapped his head pityingly. "You're nuts. For someone who doesn't like being yelled at, you sure do some dumb things." He looked around with interest. Cracks of light came through the walls of the wooden shelter and made distracting patterns on the dirt floor. Joshua peered beyond them into the shadows. He could see some stairs. "What is this place anyway?"

"A corner turret in the walls of the fort. If we climb the stairs we can see the whole fort from the lookout room."

They crept up. "Hey, this place is neat." Joshua gazed

out of a window and looked at the fort spread below. "I've only seen the outside. I didn't know all this stuff was here." He surveyed the white gravel parade ground edged with long low wooden buildings around all four sides. "So this is where all the North West Mounted Police stayed." He looked at the high wooden stockades, the lookout towers and the cannon, and started to laugh.

Danny, puzzled, looked out of the window then back at Joshua. "What's so funny?"

Joshua waved his hand around. "All this." He looked solemnly at Danny. "You guys must have been terrified of us First Nations to build stockades like this, and you know what...?"

Danny shook his head.

Joshua started to grin again. "We never attacked a fort in the whole of Alberta. The only attack this fort has seen is me." Both boys started to laugh.

"Yup," Joshua continued, "and it's some fort when you can just kick open the gate and bust in."

"OK, Big Chief," Danny chuckled, "let's see how far the invasion can get." He pointed to a building on the other side of the square. "That's where the Indian Exhibit is. If we are careful we can get there by the walkway along the top of the walls."

Joshua walked to the lookout's doorway and considered the narrow boardwalk running along the three sides of the stockade. It connected with a turret room in each corner. There was a fence on the drop side, but it wasn't solid, just a couple of sturdy rails. "Someone will see us."

"Only if we walk around," Danny pointed out. Then he grinned and nudged Joshua in the ribs. "But we're Indians, right?" He dropped to the floor and slithered out on his belly across the boards.

Joshua rolled his eyes skyward, sighed, then dropped to the floor and followed close on Danny's heels. "I've read about this in books," he grumbled in a whisper as they paused halfway to the next turret, and rubbed aching elbows and scraped knees. "I reckon it was invented by a white man."

It took ages, but eventually they wriggled into the last turret without incident and thankfully stood up inside.

They tiptoed silently down the steps and hid in the shadows again, holding their breath and listening.

Faint snatches of conversation drifted from one of the buildings.

Danny nodded with satisfaction. "They're cleaning the chapel block," he whispered to Joshua. "Sounds as though the Indian Exhibit hall is empty."

Joshua looked curiously at him. "Why are you so keen to get to that exhibit?"

"To check out the arrowheads," Danny explained. "Look." He pulled out the wad of tissues from his back pocket. "I found this, yesterday. On the reserve, just after I'd left you." He unwound the wrappings and placed the point in Joshua's outstretched palm.

Joshua sucked in his breath with admiration. "Oooh," he breathed, "It's a beaut." He looked up at Danny. "What are you going to do with it?"

Danny stared in surprise. "Keep it, of course. It's lucky."

Silently Joshua handed the point back.

"What's the matter?" Danny asked, puzzled at the sudden feeling of tension between them. "Is something wrong?"

Joshua shrugged. "Guess not. You found it." He walked to a chink in the wall and peered through it. "By the way," he threw over his shoulder, "it's a lance point, not an arrowhead."

"You know about this stuff?" asked Danny eagerly as he rewrapped the point and thrust it in his pocket. "Great, maybe we can make bows, or lances, or whatever, and play at being Indians."

"I don't have to play at being 'Indian,'" said Joshua stiffly. "I'm Peigan."

Danny stared enviously at Joshua's back. "I wish I was," he said.

Joshua turned round and looked at Danny for a long time. "No you don't," he said seriously. "Most people hate us."

Danny looked back equally seriously. "Most people hate me. They think I'm the original Ukrainian joke."

The boys stared at each other.

Suddenly Joshua stuck out his hand. "Give me five," he said.

"Give me ten," Danny instantly reacted by slapping his palm firmly on top of Joshua's. Then they thumped each other on the back until they were breathless and coughing.

"Shhh," Danny gasped, "someone will hear us." He poked his head out of the doorway and looked around. "Come on. If we're going to do this let's get on with it."

Joshua nodded and sidled up behind him. "OK" he whispered. "Say when."

Danny paused and listened again. "Now!"

The boys crept carefully around the corner of the exhibit building and and then raced up to the front door. Danny lifted the old latch. The door opened and they slid silently inside.

Chapter Six

"It's spooky here," whispered Joshua.

A dim red light from the EXIT sign above the door cast an eerie glow on their faces and hands, and made everything else dissolve into dark mysterious shadows.

Unexpectedly Danny gave a low chuckle. "Hey, did you watch that green slime movie last night?"

Joshua nodded. "Yup. Why?"

"Well, here comes the Red Slime!" Danny raised his arms above his head and advanced monster fashion towards Joshua.

There was a clang and a rattle and the sound of something slithering across the floor.

Both boys gasped and grabbed each other.

"What was that?" asked Danny.

"How would I know?" Joshua's voice wobbled.

"I think I'd better find the light switch," said Danny nervously. "I know I kicked a pail, but that slithering sound.... it was like something alive."

Joshua stood very still while Danny shuffled backwards towards the wall.

There was a sudden intake of breath.

"What's up now?" asked Joshua panicking.

"I stepped on something." Danny's voice was high and squeaky. "Something soft... I think it's dead."

Joshua groaned. "Geez, get a light on."

Danny's movements echoed uncertainly in the big room. He stretched out his hands and felt down the wall beside the door. Was the light switch on the right side or the left side of the door frame? He couldn't remember and started to feel panicky inside. Somehow this escapade wasn't fun any more. He ran his hands rapidly over the walls on both sides of the door until he felt the switch plate. "Got it!" he cried in relief.

Several fluorescent tubes flickered, then sprang to life, revealing a squashed floor cloth, an upturned pail and a slimy trail ending in a damp bar of soap.

"If it wasn't dead before, it certainly is now," said a relieved Joshua, poking the cloth with his foot.

Danny picked up the cloth and soap and dumped them in the pail. "Come on, let's check out the lance points before someone comes to pick this up." He led the way through the exhibits to the far end of the room.

They wound past cases of North West Mounted Police uniforms, and models wearing First Nations clothing. Joshua stopped and looked at them.

"Come on slowpoke." Danny grabbed his arm. "You've seen all this Indian stuff before."

Joshua shook his head. "No I haven't. I've never been here before. These clothes aren't Peigan."

Danny peered at the elaborately beaded shirt, breeches and moccasins. "Guess it's Cree. Their designs are flowers and things." He looked at Joshua for corroboration. "Don't Peigans do Blackfoot designs, patterns with squares and triangles?"

Joshua nodded, looking at Danny with interest. "How come you know that?"

"I told you I wanted to be Indian. I spent a lot of time in here last summer."

Danny headed down between the cases. "Come and look at this," he called. "It's the best thing in the whole place." And he pointed to a photo on the wall.

It was a blown up copy of a stark black and white photo showing a group of First Nations people standing in a circle, intently watching a young warrior. The young man, a dazed look on his face, was straining against two ropes tied around the top of a central pole. The end of each rope was threaded through the skin on the two fleshy parts of his chest.

"See," said Danny eagerly. "He's being tortured. They are making him pull the ropes out through his skin." He pointed to the young warrior's chest. "Do you reckon that's blood?"

Joshua glanced at the photo and turned away. "That shouldn't be here," he said flatly.

"What do you mean?" said Danny. "It's just an old photo."

"It's sacred." Joshua turned and looked at Danny. "That's the Sundance," he said fiercely. "No one's torturing him. It's a sacred ceremony." Joshua turned away again. "It's just that you people don't understand. My grandfather says the Sundance should never have been photographed."

Feeling the tension between them, Danny grappled to understand. "Sacred? You mean like in church?" he asked hesitantly.

Joshua nodded. "It's a sacred ritual. It isn't talked about and it shouldn't be photographed. Even the Sundance lodges are kept secret and are only used once."

"The lodges?" questioned Danny.

"Trees are cut and made into a circular frame, like a giant wheel. The Sundance is held inside them. Then that's the sacred site." Joshua swung around urgently to Danny. "Look, this stuff's secret. I'm only explaining so you understand. You are not to ask me anything more. OK?"

Danny nodded. "OK, but..." He hesitated. "You mean it's still going on?"

Joshua walked away.

Baffled, but not wanting to wreck his new friendship,

Danny followed Joshua. But now he wasn't sure about the stone points. Maybe Joshua would get mad when he saw them. Danny stopped in front of the case where they were displayed. "Are these sacred too?" he asked hesitantly.

Joshua walked over and looked at the display. The arrowheads and lance tips were arranged in two circles, with a couple of stone hammer heads in the middle. "Don't think so," he said, then grinned. "I don't think you'll learn anything new here. There's no information. The points have just been set out in a pretty pattern."

Danny looked critically at the display. "You're right. There's not even any dates telling how old they are." He pointed to the lower circle of arrowheads. "It doesn't even say which are arrowheads and which are lance points. Do you know?"

Joshua peered carefully through the glass. "I can tell those are lance points." He pointed to some elegant long tips arranged at the top of the circle. "The arrowheads are the small ones." He pointed to some very small tips at the bottom of the circle. "But I don't know enough to guess about the in-between sizes, they could be either. Let's see yours again."

Danny pulled out the lance tip from his pocket and the boys compared it with the ones in on display.

"It doesn't look like any here," said Danny doubtfully. "I guess it's an in-between size. Where will I find out?"

Joshua looked thoughtfully at Danny. "Have you ever been to Head-Smashed-In Buffalo Jump? To the Interpretive Centre?"

Danny shook his head. "I wanted to go last summer," he said sadly, "but we couldn't. There were so many tourists in town we all had to work in the store."

"Could you get a lift out there next weekend?"

"I might be able to, why?"

"My grandfather and my mom work there," said Joshua proudly. "My mom will know about the lance point."

"OK, I'll try and come. Saturday or Sunday?"

"Saturday," replied Joshua. "I'll be there all day." He

looked around uneasily. "I heard something. Come on, let's get out of here before someone comes."

Too late. The door at the far end opened.

"Darn," said a voice. "I thought I'd switched those off."

There was a clink of the pail, a faint click of a switch and they were plunged into pitch darkness as the door slammed.

"Hey, Danny, I can't see anything. How will we get out?" Joshua's voice had a distinct note of panic in it.

Danny stuck out his arm and waved it around until he hit Joshua's body. "It's OK, I know the way back. We'll just have to make sure we don't knock anything over." He placed Joshua's hand on his shoulder. "Don't let go. We'll take small steps and feel our way past the displays, to the exit."

They shuffled blindly in the darkness. Going past the display cases was fine, but brushing past the plaster models wearing clothes scared both of them.

"Yuk, they feel like dead bodies," whispered Danny.

"Shut up, I don't want to know," said Joshua. "Just get us out of here." He tripped on a low riser, stumbled and fell heavily on his knees. Something rocked and fell.

"Darn it... I hope nothing's broken." Danny helped Joshua up. "Come on."

They twisted and turned uneasily through what seemed like an endless maze until a final corner brought them within the glow of the red exit light. Thankfully, both boys rushed for the door and flung it open.

Their nerve gone, they slammed it behind them and raced down the boardwalk.

"This way," yelled Danny and he sped around a building, through a gap and onto a grassy field beside the fort. "Come on, over the fence."

They raced across the grass and leaped up the fence, digging their toes into the chain links. Swinging across the top almost in unison, they dropped breathlessly down on the other side.

"Hey, what do you think you're doing?" The shout was

faint behind them. They dodged down a back alley and out onto a street beyond.

"Look cool," Danny whispered out of the side of his mouth. Both boys slowed down to an easy walk and turned back into Main Street.

A truck stridently honking drew level. "Hey Joshua, move it. We've been looking all over for you," called a young woman hanging out of the truck window. "Jump in the back, we've gotta go."

Joshua ran to the truck and climbed over the tail gate. "See you next week," he called as the truck accelerated off in a cloud of exhaust fumes.

Danny wandered happily back to the store. Now he had something to look forward to next weekend. All he had to do first was survive the week at school.

Chapter Seven

Monday mornings were always bad, but this was the worst ever. Danny's head ached, so did his stomach. His eyes felt gritty and his tongue tasted awful.

"Seven-thirty," called his father, banging on the bedroom door.

"I don't feel good," Danny protested and buried his head in the pillow.

His father opened the door and looked thoughtfully at him. "Bad night, eh?"

Danny grunted in agreement.

It hadn't been easy to fall asleep. He'd heard his parents talking late into the night and he knew they were discussing his problems. He'd tossed and turned, worrying about what they were saying. Then he worried about the kids at school and what they would say. "I wish other kids liked me," Danny had muttered in the darkness as he tossed and turned. "Maybe Mom was right. I should see if Mike is interested in my den. I'll invite him over tomorrow."

With a faint sense of having resolved something, Danny had finally drifted off to sleep, but then the dreams started. Not 'the chase' one, but dreams with twenty-foot-high principals and teachers all yelling at him. Even the lance point under his pillow hadn't helped stop those.

Now, being awake was worse. He had to go and see the principal for real. His stomach muscles clenched painfully. He groaned and curled up on his side.

"You'll feel better when you've faced up to the situation, son," said his father patting his feet clumsily. "Be a man. Explain to Mr. Hubner. He is trying to help."

Danny rolled over and gazed miserably at his father. "Oh yeah, and what about Mr. Berg?"

"Danny, we all have teachers we don't like, you just have to get along with them. Running away doesn't solve anything, it just prolongs it."

Danny wished his father would shut up. He quit listening and tried to concentrate on how he was going to make himself get out of bed, face breakfast, walk out of the house and climb into the school bus.

His father looked questioningly at Danny. "Well? Will that help?"

Danny guiltily realized his father had finished talking and he didn't have a clue about the question. He rubbed his eyes. "I'm still not awake Dad, run that by me again."

"Would a ride to school help?"

Danny nodded, relieved. A ride would postpone the barrage of questions from the other kids until recess.

They arrived at school early. The almost empty playground seemed endless. Danny, head down against the wind, concentrated on placing one foot in front of the other and counting how many steps it took to cross to the school door.

"Hey. Save it!" A distant yell from a group of early morning hockey players made him swing round.

A puck shot over the ground towards him. He hopefully stuck out his foot but missed. The puck skittered past and plopped into a large puddle of dirty water.

There was a chorus of derisive groans.

"Gee, might have known. Dummy Danny! Can't you even stop a puck?" The pack of frustrated players charged over, elbowed Danny out of the way and started fishing for the puck with their sticks.

Danny ignored them and headed into the school. His stomach clenched again.

Slowly and painfully Danny bent over, took off his boots and laced on his runners. Even his extra long glow-in-the-dark laces didn't comfort him today. Carefully he stood upright and hung up his coat. He felt dead and disembodied so he concentrated on his feet. To the staccato accompaniment of his lace tips tapping on the polished floor, he watched his feet carry him down the corridor. He had never felt so small, so sick, so isolated. But no matter how slowly he walked, Mr. Hubner's office appeared to be approaching at the speed of light.

"Come in Danny," boomed Mr. Hubner. "Let's see if we can make some sense of all this."

Frozen but fascinated, Danny gazed earthward and watched his feet walk him through the principal's door and lead his body to a chair. That was when he noticed an extra set of feet. He looked up. They belonged to Mr. Berg.

Danny threw up.

The next few minutes passed in a blur. Somehow he was propelled into the staff washroom and his head held over the toilet bowl. When he'd finished retching, burly but gentle hands wiped his face with a damp cloth. His shivering body was wrapped in a blanket and he was led to a chair in the sick room.

"Feel better?" asked a voice he knew only too well.

Danny nodded, though his thoughts were in turmoil. He still felt scared and shaky but Mr. Berg... Mr. Berg had helped him. Danny looked up and for the first time in weeks, met his teacher's eyes. "Thanks," he said.

Mr. Berg drew up another chair and sat down opposite him. "Danny, you and I have to talk."

Danny nodded.

"You threw up because you were scared?"

"I dunno." Danny shifted uncomfortably. "I guess so. I couldn't help it though," he added anxiously.

Mr. Berg nodded. "You ran away because you were

scared of the mental arithmetic test, and the Social Studies project," he continued.

Danny looked at his feet again.

"So, what are you going to do about it?"

Danny eyes widened and flew up with amazement. "About what?"

"What are you going to do about being scared of me and school?"

Danny hunched resentfully back into the blanket. What could he do about anything?

Mr. Berg got up and and paced around the room. Danny watched surreptitiously. Somehow Mr. Berg trying to be nice was almost worse than Mr. Berg yelling in class. It made him feel guilty.

Mr. Berg took a deep breath and swung around. "Look Danny, there's no need to be scared. I yell and tease everyone don't I? Do I treat you any differently than the other students?"

Danny shook his head but he wasn't sure. He didn't know how many times Mr. Berg yelled at the other kids, only the times he yelled at him.

"And I only yell when you do dumb things, right?" Danny huddled miserably on the chair, hope fading. Everything he did at school someone called dumb.

Mr. Berg patted him on the shoulder. "So come on Danny, face things with courage. You're a real bright kid in some ways. You know plenty, you've got some great ideas and can express them well when you're talking. If you concentrate on your handwriting, spelling and math there is no reason why you shouldn't be in the top group. Lots of people panic in math. No big deal. Just make sure you practise your tables so that they become second nature. As for the socials project, you've got six weeks to do it. Even a grade 2 could produce it in that time. Pull yourself together and work steadily, and you and I will get along just fine."

Danny tuned out. Here was just the same old stuff. "Pull yourself together, concentrate, practice your tables and learn your spellings!" He'd heard it all before. Why did no one understand that he tried to learn all those things and it still didn't make a difference?

Danny switched over to fantasy.

Astronaut Daniel Budzynski of the Canadian Moon Base comes back to visit his school. "You're our hero," the kids yell as he strides across the school grounds. Then they cheer as he towers over Mr. Berg saying, "And I still don't know my multiplication tables."

Danny came back to the present with a jolt to find Mr. Berg towering thoughtfully over him.

"Do you find it difficult to tell me if you don't understand things?"

Danny almost laughed. Did he find it difficult? He found it impossible! What kid is going to admit he doesn't understand, to a teacher who then uses the problem as an example of how not to do things? Danny would rather die.

"Well, do you?" insisted Mr. Berg.

"You go too fast in math," mumbled Danny desperately screwing his courage to the sticking place. "I don't get it."

"Well in future come and see me at recess and I'll go over it with you. OK?"

"OK," Danny agreed uncomfortably. He'd give that a try. Being dumped on at recess was better than being dumped on in class.

The morning buzzer interrupted them. It was instantly followed by the dull roar of feet pounding through the hallways.

Mr. Hubner appeared at the office door. "All finished?" he asked brightly. "Think you can handle class, Danny?"

Danny stood up with a small sigh. He dragged off the blanket, folded it carefully and handed it to Mr. Berg. "Thanks" he said. "I'll try." And straightening his shoulders and stepping out like an astronaut, he walked determinedly down the long corridor towards the classroom door. Maybe a miracle would happen. Maybe things would be different.

Chapter Eight

The classroom noise level was worse than usual. Brett Gibson had rigged up a model helicopter hanging by a string from a stick. He was manipulating it to dive bomb the girls. They were yelling at him and covering their hair with text books.

Danny tried to sneak through to his desk unnoticed.

"Hey, the Dummy's back," announced Brett loudly and sent the helicopter swinging over Danny's head.

Stoically Danny ignored it, sat down and turned to the desk beside him. "Mike, do you want to come over tonight? I've something to show you."

"Sure." Mike looked over at Danny. "Did the IceBerg get you this morning?"

Brett Gibson gleefully dropped the helicopter so it swung between the two boy's faces.

"Come on Brett, get that thing out of here," yelled Michael over his shoulder. He turned back to Danny and lowered his voice. "Did you get a licking?"

The helicopter hung between them, humming like a malevolent wasp.

Danny shook his head. "Just a talking to." He looked at Michael and debated whether to tell him about throwing up.

The helicopter shot up in the air and then bounced lightly down on the top of Danny's head.

"Quit it Gibson," yelled Danny.

"Make me," taunted Brett, laughing and doing it again.

Angrily Danny grabbed his work book and flailed it around his head. The 'copter swung up to the ceiling out of reach.

"Aw, give up Danny. You can never hit anything anyway," laughed Brett, and buzzed Danny again.

Danny leapt onto the desk and gave a wild swing with his book. The book connected with the string and the force jerked the stick out of Brett's hand. The helicopter crashed onto a desk, drunkenly rolled over, then toppled to the floor, one blade sheared off.

The class fell silent. All eyes watched as Brett leaped up onto the desktops and advanced threateningly towards Danny.

Danny flushed. "It was his fault," he mumbled to the class at large, but stood his ground.

"Good morning Grade 5. Nice to find you quiet and ready for work." Mr. Berg strode into the room and slammed a pile of books on his desk. He looked searchingly over his glasses at the boys. "If the two mountain climbers descend, we could take out our math books and start on time for once."

Embarrassed, Danny dropped down into his seat. He hated it when Mr. Berg was sarcastic.

Brett Gibson swung down to the floor and swiftly scooped up the smashed helicopter. "I'll get you for this," he whispered as he passed Danny. "You're dead at recess." And he stomped on Danny's toe for emphasis.

"Great start to the week," thought Danny trying not to wince.

Mr. Berg launched into a geometry lesson. Danny tried to forget his other problems and concentrate on the board. To his surprise he caught on quite quickly.

"As math lessons go, this isn't too bad," he whispered to Mike, but to his surprise Mike rolled his eyes and gave a thumbs-down sign.

Heartened that he could find something easier than his friend, Danny enjoyed copying the shapes from the board onto his squared graph paper. He even managed to give the correct answer for the area of the rectangle they had drawn.

"See Danny, multiplication is easy if you concentrate, isn't it?" praised Mr. Berg, who thought Danny had multiplied the length by the width to get the answer. Danny basked in the unexpected approval, but didn't dare explain he had counted all the squares individually while Mr. Berg was talking.

Recess came far too quickly. There was an air of tension as the students streamed down the corridor. Everyone eyed Danny and Brett Gibson and waited to see who would make the first move.

Danny shot into the washroom, found an empty cubicle and slid inside, bolting the door. Then he pulled his lucky lance point out of his pocket, sat down, and turned it over and over while surveyed his options. They weren't great! He could hide in the washroom, but Brett would just wait and beat him up later. He could make an excuse to talk to Mr. Berg about the math class, but Brett would get him at lunchtime. He could try and avoid Brett Gibson, but that was almost impossible. Danny rubbed his point for luck and started on a new train of thought. When early hunters used spears they needed more than luck. They didn't just fling spears and hope to hit something, they used tactics to place themselves in a good position first. That was what he needed—tactics —a position that would take the wind out of Brett's sails. Yes, that's what he would try. With a bit of luck he could avoid a fight altogether.

Danny took a deep breath, pocketed the lance point and unbolted the cubicle door. Mike was hanging around looking anxious.

"You ready for Brett?" he asked Danny.

Danny looked unsure, but nodded. "I guess. Come on."

Danny strode across the playground, Mike close on his

heels. Furtively, other class members watched as he crossed to the far side where Brett Gibson and his gang gathered in a threatening group.

"Here comes Dummy Danny," remarked one of the group. The rest snickered. The class members closed in to watch the action. As the crowd began to grow, so did Brett Gibson's ego.

"Come to have your face smashed in, runt?" Brett started to take off his jacket.

"No. I've come to talk," replied Danny clearly.

"Then you'd better talk fast. You won't be able to after I've finished with you. You'll be cat's meat."

The crowd giggled and pressed closer.

"Look." Danny took up his stance before Brett. "Sure, you can beat me to pulp. Then what? You'll get suspended and your helicopter will still be wrecked. Right?"

Brett Gibson nodded uncertainly. He wasn't used to people facing him with reason.

"So how about I get your helicopter blade fixed?"

"Oh yeah... you and who else?"

"Me and my dad."

Brett was silent for a moment. He and everyone else know that Mr. Budzynski was great at fixing models. Mr. Budzynski won the prize for model building almost every year at Fall Fair. What's more, Danny was pretty good at fixing models himself.

Danny held his breath.

"Big deal. That helicopter was new. I only got it this weekend." Brett stepped forward, fists raised. "You wrecked it Dummy. Now you pay."

A ripple of excitement spread through the crowd.

"You're the dummy for bringing it to school," said a girl's voice. Several other girls nodded agreement.

Brett swung around angrily. "Shut your mouth Marylise, or I'll shut it for you."

"Oh yeah," taunted Marylise. "Got to beat up a girl to feel good?"

The spectators laughed.

Brett coloured angrily. This wasn't working out the way he expected. "The Dummy broke it, now he pays," he repeated.

"He's offered to fix it," Mike said. "That's fair."

"You were the one bugging him," pointed out another voice. "You were bugging us all."

Brett shifted uncomfortably. He sensed the mood of the kids had shifted. Now they were on Danny's side. He shot Danny a look of dislike. "And what if you can't fix it. Huh? What then?"

"Then we'll talk again. But I bet I can," said Danny confidently.

It was obvious to the spectators that the fight wasn't going to happen. They began to lose interest and drift away.

Brett made one last bid for power. He grabbed Danny's T-shirt, pulled it towards him and thrust his face into Danny's. "You'd better," he warned. "You'd better get it fixed real good or else..." he concentrated so hard he squinted. "Or else you won't just be cat's meat, you'll be doggy doo!" And giving Danny a push, he walked rapidly away followed by his gang.

Danny staggered back against the fence, and turned away, shoulders shaking.

Mike came over concerned. "Hey. You OK? Did he hurt you?"

Danny lifted a face creased with laughter. "No, I'm fine, I just didn't want him to see me laughing." The friends looked at each other and grinned with relief.

"Doggy doo, huh," said Mike. "We'd better watch our step." And they laughed hysterically until the bell.

Chapter Nine

School had finished for the day, but the spring afternoon had turned bitterly cold.

"Do you still want to come over?" Danny anxiously asked Mike as they sat together on the school bus. "The things I wanted to show you are outside."

"Sure." Mike grinned lazily. "It's not often you invite me to your place. I'm curious."

Danny looked at Mike uneasily. "It's nothing that special. Just a den I made." He shifted uncomfortably on the bus seat, wondering if he'd made a mistake. He almost wished he'd not offered to share his den with Mike. Mike liked games, ones with lots of body contact and excitement. Danny didn't know what a hockey fan would think about his den and he didn't want to be laughed at.

After dumping their school books in Danny's kitchen and grabbing a snack, Mike and Danny thrust their hands in their jacket pockets, hunched chins into their collars and set out across the farmyard. The sky was heavy and leaden and a few stray snowflakes drifted down. Danny stuck out his tongue to catch one.

"Where are we going?" asked Mike as they turned behind the barn and struck out across the cow pasture.

Danny grinned. "You'll see, but don't tell anyone, it's a secret place."

"I hope it's sheltered," Mike grumbled. "I'm freezing." He looked resentfully up at the sky but the sun was stubbornly hiding. He sighed and looked sideways at Danny.

Danny seemed almost oblivious to the cold. He stepped out confidently, leaning into the biting wind and heading towards the distant river valley.

Mike sighed again. He liked Danny but he was a little weird. Danny seemed to live in a world in his head that was more important than the real world. Danny made him feel uncomfortable sometimes.

"This way, but watch out, it's slippery," called out Danny, stepping over the lip of a small coulee, onto a narrow muddy cattle trail.

They carefully followed the trail down as it wound through clumps of sage and scrubby willows. Mike stopped for a moment and rubbed his aching ears. It felt good to be out of the wind.

"Come on Mike," Danny called impatiently, "or we won't have any time there. It'll be dusk soon and we'll have to head back."

Mike obediently followed and they brushed through the scrub for another few minutes, startling small animals in the undergrowth who betrayed their presence by frightened rustles. Mike looked around uneasily. He'd rather be in town, playing hockey at the rink or hanging over the video games at the convenience store. He didn't really like being out on the prairie on his own and couldn't understand Danny's fascination with it. "How much longer?" he asked impatiently.

But Danny had disappeared. Mike looked around startled.

"In here." Danny's arm shot out from a gloomy crack in the coulee wall and drew Mike through a narrow gap. "Just a minute, I'll light a candle."

It was shadowy. Mike stood still and waited for his eyes to adjust so he could see what was going on. He could hear

Danny scratching about, a sudden sputter and a tiny flame sprang to life. Carefully Danny shielded it with his hand and leaned over. The light grew as Danny lit two candles in pickle jars, placed one on a rock and held the other from a string handle attached to the jar's rim. "Well, what do you think?" he asked, holding the light up.

Mike looked around in amazement. They were standing in a dried up river channel, that widened in the middle and was blocked at the other end by a fall of rocks. The ancient river had cut deep into the bank so there was a large overhang. It was almost a cave and would be impossible to see from the fields above.

"Neat-oh," Mike breathed admiringly. "What's that?" He pointed to a large conical pile of trimmed branches nestling into the base of the cliff.

"My tipi," replied Danny proudly and walked towards it. He carefully placed the homemade lantern on the ground, shifted some concealing brush, lifted aside an old towel hanging down as a door, dropped to his knees and crawled inside. His head reappeared, framed in the doorway. "Come inside," he invited, and grabbing the lantern, disappeared from view.

Mike hesitated. "What about snakes or spiders?" he called.

"Oh for heavens sake," replied Danny crossly, "don't be chicken."

Mike pushed aside the towel and crawled through.

The tipi was just big enough for two. Rough barn planks were laid for a floor and the sloping piles of branches forming the walls were draped with old horse blankets. A cut log made a table and the pickle jar lantern swung gently from a protruding branch at the apex of the roof. The candle light made it warm and inviting.

Danny sat cross-legged and gazed anxiously at Mike. "Well, what do you think?"

Mike settled himself. "It's great. This whole place is a great secret. No one would ever find it," he enthused. "You could hide out here for weeks if you had food, but..." he hesitated and looked curiously across at Danny. "What do you do here?"

"Oh, stuff," replied Danny vaguely. "Indian stuff mostly."

Mike teasingly punched Danny on the arm. "Yeah, I forgot, you want to be Indian." He started a Hollywood style chant. "Pow pow wow wow. Pow wow wow wow," he warbled, stamping his foot and waving an imaginary tomahawk. "Come on Danny. Let's have a Sundance."

Danny froze. "It's not like that," he muttered. "And you shouldn't joke about the Sundance. It's sacred. It's nothing to do with us."

"So what, we're only having fun." Puzzled, Mike looked at Danny. "Come on man, relax. Don't be so weird. What kind of stuff do you do?"

Danny reached behind him and brought out a small rag bundle. He untied the ends and spread it out on the log. Mike gazed with bemusement at a pile of rock chips.

"See," said Danny picking up a small rock flake and holding it out to Mike. "I'm trying to make a stone point, but I can't get the shape right." He fiddled in his pocket, brought out the wad of tissues and carefully unwrapped his lance point. "It should look something like this."

"Wow!" Mike eagerly grabbed the point.

"Hey, careful," Danny gasped. "Don't break it!"

"I won't," said Mike scornfully. "I'm not a klutz. Hey! How much?"

Danny sat back on his haunches in dismay. "How much?" he faltered.

"Yeah. I'll buy this from you. How much?"

Danny shook his head, wishing he'd never shown the point to Mike. He held out his hand. "Give it back, Mike. It's mine. I'm not selling."

"Aw come on Danny, everything has a price. Two bucks, Five bucks?"

Danny shook his head again. "Come on Mike. Give it back." He leaned over the log and grabbed for it.

Mike swung his hand back laughing and held the lance

point just out of Danny's reach. "Come on Danny, name your price... I know... I'll swap you something."

"No way." Danny's voice sharpened. "I found that point myself. It's special, real special. Give it back."

The changed note in Danny's voice made Mike uncomfortable. There was something he didn't understand here. It was almost like Danny thought the Indian stuff was holy or something.

The two boys locked gazes in the candle light. Danny's eyes were as bright and fierce as an eagle's, his body ready to pounce and his hand curled into a claw. Mike shifted, ill at ease, and almost threw the point on the log. "OK, OK," he muttered. "No need to get mad."

Silently Danny picked up the point, examined it for damage and carefully wrapped and replaced it in his jeans. "We'd better go," he said abruptly, stood up and unhooked the jar from the roof, then held back the door curtain.

Mike scrambled out into the gloom. The sun had set and the dull day had settled into enveloping grayness. Mike stumbled, disoriented by the shadows.

Danny followed, carefully replacing the brush over the doorway to hide the towel. He lifted the lantern and guided Mike through the crack and out into the coulee.

"Wait here," Danny said. "I've got to put away the candles," and he disappeared.

Mike shivered, not just with the chill. The coulee was eerie, full of rustles and crackles. In the gaps between wind gusts Mike could hear the steady lap of the Oldman River, and the croak of frogs. He didn't mind the noises he knew, but what else was out there? He wished Danny would hurry up.

Danny reappeared silently. "Promise not to tell about my den."

"Cross my heart and hope to die," replied Mike promptly, matching his words with the appropriate gesture.

Danny led the way up the coulee trail. Mike followed, uneasily checking each shadow for wild animals and other things best unmentioned.

Danny too was uneasy. His relationship with Mike had changed. Both boys were relieved when they arrived back at the farm and found Mike's mother was waiting to drive him home.

Danny lay in bed that night and thought things over. "Mike should have laid off the lance point. It's mine. I found it, like I'd been meant to find it. Besides, it should be kept safe. Indian stuff's important."

Danny felt under his pillow and gently fingered the lance point. Despite the dark, each dent and chip under his fingertip painted a picture in his imagination, each flake vividly told him part of its story. As his fingers followed the shape, his imagination wove a dream.

A young hunter sat in the shade of a shallow coulee, painstakingly and lovingly knapping the point. It was a long job. The hunter wasn't an expert, he worked slowly and carefully, feeling his way a flake at a time, till the delicate shape emerged, sharp and beautiful, born out of stone. The hunter stood up and triumphantly held the lance point in the air and watched the sunbeams glance off the translucent edges. Then when it seemed to glow and absorb the sunlight, the hunter knelt down and bound it firmly onto a long straight stick. Grasping the stick he swiftly walked up the coulee. As he reached the coulee rim, the hunter paused for a moment, silhouetted against the sky. He had one eagle feather in his head band.

Smiling happily at the image he'd created, Danny drifted off to sleep.

Chapter Ten

The school week settled into its usual routine and Danny muddled through. Stoically, he accepted difficult situations, and dealt with them the best way he could, by losing himself in daydreams.

His favourite daydream lasted right through one Socials period.

Barenaked Ladies' touring bus broke down outside the school. Danny helped them fix the engine. The Barenaked Ladies were so grateful they did a free concert in the school gym. All the students loved the music and danced and rocked for hours. The teachers hated it and tried to get the speakers turned down. Eventually the roof couldn't take the blast from the speakers and started to crack and all the roof beams bent out of shape. School was closed for good. Danny was a hero. "You don't need school anyway," said the Barenaked Ladies, "but we need a 'Mr. Fix-It'. Come on the road with us and fix our equipment." So he did and became rich and famous.

By that time Socials period was over.

Each evening Danny took out his calendar and crossed off the days to the weekend. Each morning he doggedly arrived at school. He was totally surprised if something pleasant happened during a school day.

Friday was a surprise.

"Today is the day you get one hour's project research time in the library," announced Mr. Berg with a big smile.

Danny sat up straight in his desk. Great. He liked working in the library. He'd chosen his favourite topic—'Indians'—and knew where there were a couple of books he could look at.

"By the end of the afternoon I want you to each hand in a one-page outline of your project," continued Mr. Berg. "It should start with a clear and concise explanation of your project, about one paragraph in length. Underneath the paragraph, in point form, list the topics or chapters you will be covering."

The whole class groaned, Danny's groan was loudest and he slumped back in his seat.

Mr. Berg looked in his direction with a frown. "What's the matter Danny, don't you have a project?"

"I do Mr. Berg. Honest I do," Danny stammered. "I've been working on it all week. I've a collection of post cards and I know lots of stuff and I've talked to people. It's just..." he tailed off, wondering how he was going to organize and write it all down so that Mr. Berg could read it.

"Well if you've done all that, you've got a head start," Mr. Berg said briskly. "Line up by the door, Grade 5, and walk quietly to the library."

Danny sat miserably at his library table. He had tons of information in his head. He'd organized his picture post-card card collection in a box at home ready to illustrate his report. The cards showed scenes of early life on the prairie, Indian encampments, tipi rings and the Indian clothing displays in the Fort Macleod museum. He had his lance point. He planned on painting a picture of the young hunter he had imagined knapping the flint point. He had met a real Indian kid and his grandfather and was going to visit Head-Smashed-In Buffalo Jump with them. Danny's project was all set to go. Except that he had to write it!

Danny looked around the library in despair. It was quiet, much quieter than usual as his whole class had their heads down at the tables, scribbling away furiously in order to hand their outlines in on time. Mr. Berg was looking pleased and talking to the librarian in a low voice.

"This is just what this class needs," Mr. Berg murmured in a satisfied tone. "A project that they can get their teeth into. They are a bright bunch on the whole apart from..." He stopped and his eyes swept the room and locked with Danny's.

Danny flushed scarlet, bent his head down and crooked an arm protectively over his paper. He knew what Mr. Berg had been going to say—'apart from Danny'. He looked sadly at the paper in front of him. It was black and smudged with eraser marks, crossings out and badly scrawled words written several times in an effort to spell them correctly. He sighed. Why was it so difficult to organize his thoughts and knowledge into a one-page outline when it was stuff he knew?

Footsteps approached and the hair on the back of his neck prickled. Sure enough Mr. Berg's hand expertly whisked the paper from his desk.

"'INJUNS'" Read out Mr. Berg loudly.

The class grinned and sat back ready to enjoy the joke.

"'INJUNS ARE VERY UNTRIST / INTRUST / INTERESTING'— very good Danny, third time lucky."

The class giggled. Danny squirmed praying that Mike wouldn't let on he'd told Danny how to spell 'interesting.'

"INTERESTING PIPILL / PEOPUL / PEEPUL," continued Mr. Berg. "THEY LIVE ON RISURVS AND GO TO SCOOL LIKE US BUT THEY YUST TO LIV A DIFERENT LIF." He stopped and looked down at Danny. "Need I go on?"

Danny shook his head and looked down at his table.

"And what should Danny be using?" questioned Mr. Berg loudly.

"His dictionary," chorused the class.

"Did you bring your dictionary with you?" asked Mr. Berg.

Danny shook his head again.

Mr. Berg dropped Danny's paper on the table, walked over to a shelf and pulled out a boxed set of two of the biggest, thickest books Danny had ever seen. He slapped them down in front of Danny. "This is a dictionary. Go on. Open it Danny."

Danny clumsily pulled one of the heavy volumes out of its box and opened a page at random. It was full of tiny writing. Danny had never seen so many words packed together on one page. They danced and wriggled and swirled around like a whirlpool and tried to suck him inside and swallow him. Danny leaned back in horror.

"Guess how many words in that book," ordered Mr. Berg.

"I dunno. Millions?" gasped Danny.

"Probably," agreed Mr. Berg. "These two books make the Concise Oxford Dictionary. It is one of the best dictionaries in the world, and our school is lucky to own one. Despite its enormous size, in order to fit in almost ALL the words of the English language, it is printed in such tiny lettering that most people need this to help them read it." Mr. Berg dropped a large Sherlock Holmes-type magnifying glass on top of the page.

"Hey, neat." Several kids came and crowded round Danny's table.

"Can I look up a word Mr. Berg?" asked Marylise, grabbing the magnifying glass.

"Mr. Berg, does that dictionary have swear words in?" asked Brett Gibson interestedly.

Mr. Berg ignored him and looked over his glasses at Danny. "Do you ever use your school dictionary, Danny?"

Danny shrank down in his seat and shook his head. How could he explain he got lost in dictionaries?

"Why not?"

"I can never find the words in them." Danny whispered, ashamed.

Someone laughed. "That's what they're for, dummy."

Mr. Berg glared around and the laughter subsided.

Danny stuttered defensively. "If... if... " he took a deep

breath. "If you don't know how to spell the word, how can you find it in the dictionary?"

Mr. Berg rolled his eyes. "Then we'll go through it again. Let's find the word 'reserve' in this dictionary."

To Danny's horror, the magnifying glass was thrust into his hand, the giant dictionary pushed under his nose, and the entire class crowded around to help.

"MR. BERG, COULD YOU SEND DANNY BUDZYNSKI TO THE OFFICE IMMEDIATELY, DANNY BUDZYNSKI, THANK YOU."

The announcement over the school loudspeaker galvanized Danny to action. He dropped the magnifying glass as though it was red hot, pushed back his chair and shot through the crowd of students as though propelled from a cannon. Heaving a sigh of relief, he raced up the corridor and screeched to a halt in the office. He didn't know what was waiting for him there. But it had to be better than that kid-eating dictionary.

"Ah Danny," boomed Mr. Hubner, as he put the loud speaker mike back on its stand. "That was quick."

"We were in the library," explained Danny breathlessly.

"Well come on in. There is someone who would like to meet you."

Mystified, Danny followed Mr. Hubner to his office, then stopped short at the door when he saw his mother. "Oho," he thought, "what have I done now?" Much to his relief she smiled reassuringly at him. He looked at the principal again.

"Danny, this is Ms. Wakefield. She's a friend of your mother who works with students who have learning problems."

The tiniest woman Danny had ever seen stepped from behind Mr. Hubner's bulk. Danny blinked. He was considered tall for his age, but most adults still towered over him. Not this woman, though. She was just about his height.

She smiled and held out her hand. "Hi Danny. I'm Carol Wakefield. I'm really pleased to meet you."

Danny automatically took her hand and shook it, then

looked questioningly around at the other adults. What was going on? His Mother didn't usually bring visitors to meet him at school.

Mr. Hubner pointed to a row of three chairs. "Sit down Danny. We'd like to talk to you for a minute."

Danny perched uncomfortably on the chair next to his mother, her friend sat on his other side and Mr. Hubner sat behind his desk.

Mr. Hubner cleared his throat. "Danny, you've been having some problems doing your school work."

Danny's heart sank. He nodded and looked miserably down at the floor. He might have known he'd be in trouble again.

"Well it seems that er... Ms... er... Wakefield here, works with students who are experiencing problems," Mr. Hubner continued. "She'd like you to take some tests. Then when the results come through she might have some suggestions that would help you."

Danny froze. In fact he had heard only one word—TEST. It echoed and rolled around the inside of his head, emptying his brain of all knowledge, shrinking him, and leaving him hollow and shaky.

From miles away the adults seemed to be looking expectantly at him.

Help came from an unexpected quarter. The woman next to him turned, gently touched her hand to his knee and looked reassuringly at him. "Not those kind of tests," she said gently. "Not school tests. My tests are more like games, really. You can't fail them Danny—no one can."

Danny looked at her in amazement and the room slowly slid back into focus. This woman could read his mind. She knew he had frozen at the word 'test'. Maybe, just maybe, she could understand his problems.

"How come I can't fail?" asked Danny suspiciously.

"There's nothing to fail, it's just exercises to show me how your brain works."

"I'll fail," said Danny positively. "My brain doesn't work."

Everyone laughed as though he'd cracked the joke of the century. Danny wriggled uneasily.

"Not true, Danny," said Ms. Wakefield with a twinkle. "This morning your mom showed me some models you'd assembled. How did you make those models?"

"I just followed the diagrams," said Danny baffled.

Ms. Wakefield nodded. "Yes. Your brain decoded the picture and you were able to figure it out and stick all the pieces together in the right order. You've a good brain Danny. If you do the exercises, I'll be able to see the ways your brain works, the skills you've got. Then maybe we can figure out some ways to use those skills in school." She paused and looked consideringly at him. "Think about it Danny, but you don't have to do them if you don't want to."

A small sputter of surprise escaped Mr. Hubner. Everyone turned to look at him. But before he could speak Ms. Wakefield spoke again.

"Yes, these exercises are voluntary." she said firmly. She looked back at Danny, "and no one will be mad at you if you decide you don't want to take them. It's your choice."

"Are they long tests?" asked Danny thoughtfully.

Ms. Wakefield smiled wickedly. "There's several. You'd probably miss class for the rest of today."

Danny's brain worked overtime. Reprieve. If he spent the day doing these dumb tests, then Mr. Berg couldn't expect him to hand in his project outline. Then he'd get the weekend to work on it in peace and his mom could help him with the spelling.

"I'll do them," he said, and he and Ms. Wakefield grinned conspiratorially at each other.

His mother sighed with relief. "Good for you Danny," she whispered.

Mr. Hubner stood up. "The sick room is empty. If we moved a table and a couple of chairs in there could you use that?"

"Perfect," said Ms. Wakefield with a smile. "Let's go, Danny. It's time to prove to yourself how smart you really are."

Chapter Eleven

The sick room was bare, cold looking, and smelled of disinfectant. A small camp bed with a worn looking blanket folded across the bottom of a lumpy mattress was the only furniture.

Ms. Wakefield wrinkled her nose. "Bet no one wants to be ill in your school," she commented quietly to Danny as they waited for the janitor to finish dragging a table and two chairs in from the corridor.

Danny grinned. "We call this the jail," he confided.

"I'm not surprised." Thanking the curious janitor, Ms. Wakefield firmly closed the door, set the chairs on opposite sides of the table, organized her briefcase beside her, and motioned Danny to sit down. "First of all, I'm not your teacher and this room is not the classroom. I'm your Mom's friend, I'd like to be yours, and my name's Carol. OK?"

Danny nodded and sat down, nervously twisting and untwisting his legs around the chair legs.

Carol grinned encouragingly at him. "So, Danny why don't you tell me about school."

Danny shrugged uncomfortably. "Not much to tell. I just hate it."

"Why?"

Danny shrugged again. "I guess... because I don't do things right... I don't try hard enough, so everyone gets mad at me."

Carol looked thoughtfully at him. "You don't try hard enough. Is that what you say or what your teacher says?"

Danny's eyes flew up to her face. She smiled encouragingly.

"That's what everyone says," Danny muttered, dropping his eyes to the table and twisting his legs uncomfortably the other way.

"Everyone?"

Danny nodded. "Even the kids. They think I'm stupid."

Carol's voice was very gentle. "And what about you Danny? Is that what you think?"

There was a long pause.

A roller coaster of thoughts rushed around Danny's head. What did he think? He thought something in his head was wrong because he couldn't write or do math. He thought about the dictionary and Mr. Berg. All the hockey pucks and baseballs he missed catching flashed through his mind. His ears rang with customer's annoyed complaints because he'd given wrong change in the store, and he saw his father's angry face when he read all the 'must try harder' remarks on Danny's report card. All his failures crashed and rolled around his head and almost overwhelmed him.

"Well Danny, what do you think?" Carol's voice was quietly insistent.

"I think I've got a brain tumor or something," Danny said very quietly. "I think my brain is sick."

The words hung heavy in the air.

Danny didn't dare look at Carol. That was the dumbest thing he'd ever said. She'd laugh.

Two small hands reached out across the table and grabbed his hands tightly. "Look at me, Danny Budzynski." Carol's voice was urgently compelling.

Danny looked up with haunted eyes.

She squeezed his hands tighter. "That's your nightmare, isn't it Danny? That you've got a brain tumor or something else really awful?"

He nodded.

"Danny. I used to think that about myself. Know what?" She urgently jiggled his hands till he responded.

Danny automatically shook his head.

"I'm grown up and I still can't spell."

Danny dully gazed across at Carol.

"Yes," she continued. "I was like you only my nightmare was that I must be adopted. I figured that must be why I was the only dumb one in my family and why they all yelled at me when I couldn't do things."

"But you can do things now," Danny stammered.

Carol shook her head. "No, there's lots of things I still have difficulty with. But I wasn't adopted and I didn't have a brain tumor. I have a learning disability; my brain short-circuits."

Danny looked blank. "Huh?"

"Have you ever used a computer, Danny?"

"Yup, my dad's. I play games on it sometimes."

"Has it ever 'glitched' on you Danny? Had a fault in the program?"

Danny grinned slowly. "You bet. Once we had this new game and when we tried to boot it up it kept saying 'Disk Error'. Dad got real mad."

"Well, my brain has one or two disk errors on it."

Danny looked at Carol in disbelief. "But you're at the university. You're a 'brain'."

Carol grinned wickedly. "I am now. But at school I was bottom of the class. Now I specialize in helping kids who are struggling with some of the same problems I had." Carol gave Danny's hands one more comforting squeeze before dropping them. "There's no brain tumor, Danny but your brain might be glitching. Want to see if we can figure it out?"

"Can you fix it?" asked Danny hopefully.

Carol looked seriously across at him. "I don't know. But if we can figure out what's wrong we might be able to find some ways around it." She grinned. "Kind of like reprogramming you."

Danny laughed and felt the tension beginning to flow out of him. He uncurled his legs and relaxed a little more into his seat.

Carol rummaged in her briefcase and pulled out some papers and a box. "These games will tell me what you're really good at as well as where you are having difficulty. Won't it be neat if we can show your teacher and the other kids your skills? Explain all the things you are good at."

"I guess so." Danny was doubtful. "But what if I'm good at nothing?"

Now it was Carol's turn to look surprised. "But we already know you are good at some things. Don't forget your mom showed me all these models you'd built. Now that's a real gift."

"Oh that stuff." Danny squirmed in his chair. "I mean stuff that really counts."

"It'll count," said Carol with confidence. "You'll see." And she tipped a box of brightly patterned wooden cubes across the table.

"Here's the first game." She handed Danny a card with a pattern printed on it. "Want to see if you can make that pattern with those cubes?"

Danny glanced at scattered cubes and then at the pattern in his hand. It seemed like kid stuff. "I guess so."

"Right," said Carol, "but to make it more fun I'm going to time how fast you do it." She pulled out a stop watch. "Start when I say 'go'. Tell me when you're ready."

Danny propped the card up where he could see it and poised his hands above the cubes.

"Ready?" asked Carol.

"Ready," he replied looking at the cubes.

"GO."

Danny's fingers flew. He turned and pushed and rolled the cubes, checked with the card, and in no time at all there was the pattern on the table in front of him.

"Wow! You're fast," said Carol admiringly as she clicked off the stop watch and entered the time in a small book. "Want to try a more difficult one?"

They sorted the cubes several times, then looked at pictures, and sorted them into an order that told a story. They played games with numbers and words and laughed a lot. Danny even relaxed enough to do some spelling and math for Carol.

"Phew! Is that recess already?" Danny asked Carol in surprise as the school buzzer interrupted them.

"Oh no," Carol laughed. "That's the final buzzer. It's home time. You've worked all afternoon."

"Wow. I didn't know school could go so fast," remarked Danny. "What happens now?"

"You go home and enjoy your weekend," Carol stuffed the papers and equipment into her briefcase. "I'll look at everything you've done and get back to you some time next week." She looked up at Danny. "You've worked really hard Danny. You should be proud of yourself."

"Have I passed?" said Danny eagerly.

Carol laughed. "Remember what I said?"

"You can't pass or fail on this," Danny chanted along with her.

"Right. You've done well, Danny. Believe me?"

"OK." Danny grinned back. "It was fun. 'Bye Carol." And he ran to catch the school bus.

He slouched, happy and relaxed, in the bus seat, turning his lance point over in his pocket. The luck seemed to be working. Today hadn't been that bad. Carol was nice, his mom could help him with his project outline, and tomorrow was Saturday and the visit to Head-Smashed-In Buffalo Jump. Things were looking up.

Chapter Twelve

Saturday was a perfect T-shirt and cut-off day. In true prairie fashion, spring had whisked into summer overnight. It was hot.

Danny, on the lookout for Joshua, excitedly hung out of the car window as his mother swung into the entrance of Head-Smashed-In Buffalo Jump Interpretive Centre.

"There doesn't seem to be anyone around," remarked his mother doubtfully.

"Joshua'll be here," Danny said confidently and leapt from the car. "Anyway I can always phone you if there's a problem."

His mother nodded and drove off.

PUM pom pom pom, PUM pom pom pom. Distant drums caught Danny's attention as his mother's car roared away. Insistently they pounded and called to him, accompanied by a high wordless song, thin as the breeze. They called from below, from beyond the road that curved up the hillside, from a patch of sunny prairie where a circle of tipis and trucks protected an arbour of tree branches and brush. He couldn't see the drums but Danny sensed they were there, hidden in the interwoven branches, enticing him nearer.

"Want to go down?" Joshua materialized soundlessly beside Danny. "The drum teams are practicing for the dance competition this afternoon."

Danny turned to say something, then stopped in surprise. This was a new Joshua; gone were the usual T-shirt and jeans, instead he wore a loose red cotton tunic belted with a leather thong, breeches and breechcloth made of navy blue blanketing and trimmed with red braid, and beautiful red and blue beaded moccasins with hide ankle wraps. This wasn't the kid Danny had hung around Fort Macleod with. This was a stranger, a Peigan Indian, an unknown quantity.

Joshua laughed. "What's the matter Danny, scared of me?"

This was so close to the truth that Danny flushed uncomfortably. "You... you just look... different."

Joshua gave him a friendly push. "Come on. You've seen outfits like this before."

Danny wobbled and teetered on the concrete ledge. "Sure I have," he countered. "In the museum." He regained his balance and grinned across at Joshua. "So, why are you wearing one? You a museum exhibit or something?"

Joshua looked at Danny consideringly. "No," he said softly, "I'm no exhibit. I'm for real. I'm a dancer."

Danny was immediately aware he had said something wrong, but he wasn't sure what. "Are you dancing today then?" he asked hesitantly.

"Yup, this afternoon, "Joshua said proudly. "At the pow wow. It's a big celebration. My people are transferring a tipi over to the Interpretive Centre. You can come if you like."

Danny was now totally out of his depth. "What do you mean, 'transferring a tipi'? Handing it over to someone?"

"No WAY! You can't just hand a tipi over," said Joshua, shocked. "Tipis have power. They have to be transferred from one person to another in a sacred ceremony."

"They do?" Danny was baffled.

"Come on, you'll see." Joshua leapt over the concrete

barrier and bounced lightly down the hillside in giant leaps that showed his familiarity with the terrain. Danny copied, leaping ever increasing distances as he gained momentum on the slope. He reached the bottom in a slither of small stones but, somewhat to his surprise, still upright.

The drumming was louder now. Danny stood and listened. The rhythms curled around him like the heartbeat of the earth.

"Come on, slowpoke." Joshua darted across the road that separated the hillside from the prairie, and dodged into the ring of tipis. Danny followed.

The tipis were large; larger than Danny had realized. Stiffly they rose from the prairie grass, a wall of giant white cones painted with vivid designs, surrounding and crowding him, protecting their territory. Then there were the people. People busy doing jobs Danny had never done, had never dreamed needed doing. A youth handled a long pole to manipulate a smoke flap way above Danny's head. A woman sat in a doorway sewing fringe onto a shawl. An older man pounded wooden tipi pegs into the ground; a team of young people, long hair streaming in the wind, coordinated to set up the tall poles to frame another tipi; a group of teenage girls laughingly hurled firewood off the back of a truck to waiting friends, and small children ran around among them all, shouting excitedly. The whole area was a hive of activity orchestrated by the pulse of drums, but Danny felt isolated. It was as though he wasn't there.

"No one looks at me," he thought uncomfortably. "I don't belong here. Where is Joshua!"

"Psst, Danny."

A sibilant whisper from low down made Danny jump.

"Come and watch. The ceremony's just starting." Joshua was kneeling in a tipi entrance. "You can sit here, in the doorway," he continued in a low voice. "But don't come inside." He tugged Danny's leg and motioned for Danny to move over and sit at the side of the doorway.

Danny knelt and looked into another world.

The books Danny read had always described the insides

of tipis as dark and smoky. But this interior was bathed in sunlight. The sun glowed through the tipi walls, illuminating the bright geometric designs on the wall liner and the intent faces of the participants. Danny was immediately aware of the fact he was watching something serious. There was a thin haze of smoke, but Danny only noticed it because of the subtle fragrance. Unconsciously he sniffed and tried to identify it.

"Sweetgrass," Joshua murmured.

The tipi was crowded. Two elderly women sat on plastic folding chairs, but most people were sitting cross-legged on blankets around the circular walls. Danny copied them, crossing his legs and straightening his back.

The grassy floor in the centre of the tipi was empty but for a shallow, sandy depression containing a small fire. A young man, wearing his hair in a single braid, knelt beside the fire and tended it with wooden tongs until it glowed steadily. Immediately opposite Danny, beyond the fire, sat Joshua's grandfather.

The stillness emanating from the old man was so complete Danny could almost touch it.

Silence hung and shimmered in the air for a long time.

With a breathy sound like a ripple of wind amongst dry leaves, the old man spoke. The language was Blackfoot, but Danny knew it was a prayer. He bowed his head and shut his eyes and let the sounds wash around and enfold him.

A feeling of movement made him open his eyes. The fire tender leaned across the tipi floor and dropped some live coals from the tongs onto a small sandy mound at the old man's feet. With almost imperceptible movements, the old man directed the hot coals be split, and minute amounts of the glowing embers placed around the rim of the sandy mound, at the four points of the compass, the rest dropped in the middle. The young man finished and sank back on his haunches by the central fire. The old man moved something carefully onto the middle coal. A thin smudge of smoke rose and the fragrance in the air grew stronger. Danny leaned forward excitedly so he could see clearly. He was witnessing the burning of a braid of sweetgrass.

The old man passed a small bone to the fire tender and the young man strode out to the tipi entrance, stepping over Danny, and raised it to his lips. A thin high whistle sounded. The young man turned North, South, East and West, each time blowing the bone whistle.

"He's inviting the world to witness the ceremony," Joshua whispered to Danny.

So many unfamiliar things slowly began to unfold that Danny lost track of what was happening. The low hum of the incomprehensible language, the slow, deliberate pace of the ceremony, the heat of the sun, all combined to put him in a trance state. He was never able to fully explain, but somehow he felt his spirit mingled and became part of the ritual. He witnessed people bathing themselves in the cleansing smoke of the sweetgrass, and accepting symbols painted on their faces and began to feel and grasp the elusive concept that somehow these people were not just being given a tipi. They were being offered a symbol of power, protection maybe, that they had to cherish and care for.

That was as close as Danny could get. He didn't know if his interpretation was right, but he knew he was witnessing something serious and important.

Without warning, the atmosphere changed. The people in the tipi smiled and chatted with each other. Blankets and quilts wrapped in plastic appeared and were presented to the elder women. The elder men were given gifts of tobacco and cigarettes.

"I guess it's over," said Danny in a somewhat dazed voice. He was suddenly aware that his legs were cramped and his back ached and that he had sat without moving for an unknown length of time.

Joshua nodded. "We can leave now. Want to see the buffalo jump before the dancing starts?"

Danny nodded, though he really wasn't sure. His senses were dulled from the bombardment of new impressions. He really would have liked to sit down quietly and think about everything he'd experienced. But he stood up stiffly and followed Joshua.

They walked back uphill, but instead of crossing the car parks and entering the building, Joshua turned aside and clambered up the steep slope beside the building. "Come on," he called. "We'll do the exhibits last. Come and see the real stuff first."

They scrambled to the top, ducked under a rail, and jogged along the ridge path to where the ground fell sharply away in a great gash. They paused, dusty and sweaty, on the cliff edge to catch their breath.

The view was magnificent.

The prairie rolled away below them. It stretched for ever. An endless sea of tawny greens and browns swirled and merged to the blue horizon. Below them, the tipi encampment looked like a paper model.

Once again Danny was aware of the wind. It rejuvenated and refreshed him. He stretched out his arms like wings and felt it tug and push at his body. "I bet this wind has travelled hundreds of miles," he said wonderingly, "just blown hundreds of miles over the prairie, and now it's blowing on us. Wonder if it's strong enough to lean on?"

Both boys stepped back from the cliff edge, found a clear space, then turned their backs and leaned slowly and gently into the constant wind. Further, further, till they fell into a laughing huddle on the ground.

Danny rolled onto his stomach and crawled forward until his head was hanging over the edge of the cliff. It was a long way down to a cruel jagged rock below. He shuddered. "I know the buffalo fell over here. But how did your people make them do it?" he asked.

"Ah... you ask the right questions, young man," said a new voice.

Embarrassed, Danny jumped to his feet, brushing the dust and grass from his clothes, and turned to face Joshua's grandfather.

"Can you tell him, Naaahsa?" asked Joshua. "He's really interested."

The old man nodded, looked around, and found a nearby rock to sit on. Both boys squatted at his feet.

"So, how did the buffalo come to this place and sacrifice themselves?"

Danny nodded.

"We called them."

There was a long silence. Danny tried to think of something to say. Was Joshua's grandfather teasing him? He looked perfectly serious, but 'calling' buffalo? Danny stirred uncomfortably but before he could speak the old man spoke again.

"My father told me of the song of the holy woman. It was a powerful song. She sang only when our people were hungry. She sang to the 'iniskim', the buffalo stone, and if she sang truly, in a time of need, the buffalo would hear her and come to us."

The old man looked out over the prairie as though seeing it in a time long past. He gestured sideways towards the low hills leading up to the buffalo jump cliff. "The runners hid up there and watched for the buffalo to appear, then they would lead them to the runs."

Danny's head was whirling. "But how?" he said exasperated. "How can you lead buffalo? I can't get our cows to move without yelling and slapping their rumps."

"Have you tried asking them, and explaining why you want their milk?"

Danny's eyes widened and he looked helplessly at the old man.

"We didn't just kill the buffalo. We asked it to sacrifice itself. And when it did, we gave thanks to its spirit, asked for forgiveness, and we wished the herd well. When the herd came to us, the runners dressed as wolves and crept through the grass towards them. The herd would edge away. So carefully and with great skill, the people would entice the buffalo nearer and nearer the runs."

Though he was still finding some aspects difficult to grasp, Danny tried to hang in. "The runs," he asked urgently, "what runs?"

The old man picked up a stick and drew a line in the

dust at his feet.

"Here is the cliff edge... the jump... where we are sitting."

Danny nodded his comprehension.

The old man placed the tip of this stick firmly in the centre of the line. "The buffalo had to run towards the edge here to fall over."

Danny nodded.

The old man made a series of dots in a V shape with the bottom of the V right on the line. "So the people used the natural valleys and heaps of stones to make a series of runs or funnels that encouraged the buffalo to stampede towards the jump." He stood up and stretched his arms in front of him in a wide V.

"But how?" asked Danny persistently.

"Well, everyone had their job. While the runners were edging the buffalo towards the runs, the rest of the people were also making preparation. Some of them hid behind the rock cairns. When the buffalo appeared the people startled them by leaping up and waving and shouting. The buffalo would then turn away and stampede in the only direction that seemed clear, down the runs. Those that were brave and fast would sacrifice themselves over the jump."

Danny sat spellbound. He could imagine it all.

The buffalo grazed peacefully on the prairie grass, unaware of a man on all fours, a wolf hide draped over his head and shoulders, a man who copied the stalking movements of the wolf. The herd of great brown giants smelled only the hide and edgily moved away from their enemy the wolf... further... and further... into the mouth of the man-made funnel. Suddenly there was a great SHOUT! From behind a mound of rocks, people jumped up noisily waving sticks and flags. The same from the other side and another mound, then another. The buffalo were surrounded and frightened by the noise and commotion. There was only one clear escape route, forward. Panicked, the giant herd began to run. Hooves pounded the ground. Breath came in pants and gasps. Tiny eyes staring, the buffalo poured down the narrowing fun-

nel. They came in a great roaring brown tide that made the earth shake. The tide foamed over the edge of the jump and crashed on the rocks below.

As the roaring in his head died away, Danny realized Joshua was staring at him. "It's OK," Danny explained with a grin. "I was just seeing it in my head."

The old man smiled. "You have the inner eyes," he commented gently. "That is a wonderful gift."

"That's the second time this week I've been told I had a gift," said Danny in amazement. "I didn't think I was good at anything."

"Everyone has a gift," said the old man, "but some take a while to find it." He looked seriously across at Danny. "Use your gift well."

"OK." Danny wasn't sure how else to respond. Using his imagination was something that usually got him into trouble. He'd have to think about that one.

KEEPERS

Chapter Thirteen

Stiffly the old man rose to his feet. The boys followed and together they walked along the ridge path to the upper entrance of the Interpretive Centre. Danny hung back a little. He found himself reluctant to go inside the building.

"What's the matter Danny? Don't you want to see the exhibits?" Joshua was puzzled.

"Well yes, kind of." Danny struggled to identify his feelings. "It's just that... a building..." He made a wide sweeping gesture that encompassed the jump and the magnificent view, and the pictures his inner eyes had conjured up. "It's just that THIS... it's great. You can't put things like this in a building." He scanned the scene thoughtfully. "After watching a real Indian ceremony and then seeing the Buffalo Jump, I'm scared that the exhibits will be a letdown," he continued honestly.

The old man smiled gently but said nothing.

Joshua punched Danny's arm. "Aw come on, you're just being weird. The Interpretive Centre is full of neat stuff. Did you bring the lance point?"

Danny nodded and patted the back pocket of his cutoffs.

Joshua led the way through the doors of the Interpretive Centre, pressed a button for the elevator and the three of them travelled down to the exhibit levels.

Danny wandered happily on his own through the displays. Joshua was right, there were wonderful things to be discovered. Peigan stories of the creation of the earth; explanations of the native names for the seasons; the use of herbs and wild foods that Danny had never realized could be eaten; clothing, fire making, drums and rattles. Danny even found a magical 'iniskim'—the buffalo stone.

"I wonder if you're the one the holy woman sang to when she called the buffalo," Danny whispered as he bent down and looked at it with awe.

The iniskim was small, black and buffalo-shaped. Its well-polished surface gleamed dully as though it had been rubbed and handled during many years of ceremonies. Danny could feel the power pulsing from it. His head whirled and he had to turn away.

"Holy Comoly," he gasped.

There they were... just as if they'd been 'called' by the Holy Woman... just exactly as he'd imagined them.... A magnificent group of buffalo poised on the edge of the reconstructed jump, buckling at the knees and frozen in time as they were about to topple over to their deaths.

"WOW!" Danny went closer and looked at the brown muscular beasts whose shoulders towered above him. "You're massive."

Even stuffed and on display the buffalo emanated power and strength. Danny leaned over the barrier to stroke the rough hairy hide.

"Don't touch the exhibits!" A brisk looking woman in a red jump suit called out sharply as she walked through the gallery. Danny blushed and moved back quickly but still stared at the animals.

"The buffalo were our strength." Behind Danny, the old man appeared again and spoke quietly. "That is why we honour them. We wasted nothing that the buffalo gave us. Without them...?" the old man's voice died away.

Danny grappled to understand the undercurrents he could sense behind the old man's speech. "But YOU didn't die out, only the buffalo. You still have tipis and language and ceremonies. Even the Sundance." He gulped as he remembering it was a forbidden subject. "I'm sorry," he stammered, embarrassed. "I just... it always fascinated me... in the Fort Macleod museum."

"Ah yes. The photograph on display. Joshua told me." The old man moved over to a seat and motioned for Danny to join him.

"In all cultures there are differences, and in First Nations cultures there are some things that white people find hard to understand." The old man spoke seriously but without anger. "We believe that some things should not be shown or explained. This includes the sacred ritual of the Sundance. We do not talk about it. The sites are sacred sites... hidden from eyes that don't understand. The ritual is secret and holy. It should have never been photographed. In your society you have anthropologists, people who try and discover our rituals and explain them. But we are people, not interesting animals to be studied and explained. We are a people. We have sacred beliefs we choose not to share."

Danny sat quietly, trying to marshall his muddled thoughts to explain his point of view to the old man. "See... see... it's hard not to be nosey," Danny stammered earnestly. "Like... I'm real interested. I want to know everything and see everything. And the sacred stuff's the most interesting." Danny paused, grappling for words.

The old man waited patiently.

"I guess it's hard to understand because in our culture we don't have anything that holy," Danny said slowly.

"Some of you do," said the old man gently. "Do you go to church Danny, to Mass?"

Danny shuffled uncomfortably. "Mom does, but Dad and I don't go very often," he admitted. "Actually, just once or twice a year, like Christmas," he added honestly.

"What about the wafers and wine?" questioned the Old

Man. "Could they be taken and displayed in a museum?"

"Oh no," said Danny definitely, "They're holy... they're consecrated." He stopped suddenly, realizing the impact of his statement. "You mean that's kinda like the Sundance?"

The old man eased himself out of the seat, nodded at Danny and left. Danny stared after him.

Joshua appeared around the corner.

"I think I've offended your grandfather," said Danny unhappily, and he explained what had happened.

"It's OK," Joshua reassured him. "The elders like to leave you to work things out for yourself."

"Sheesh..." Danny's breath expelled slowly. "If the Sundance ceremony is really sacred..." He shook his head as if to clear it. "Joshua, that photo shouldn't be in the museum. I wonder if we can do anything about it?"

Chapter Fourteen

Before Joshua could answer, he caught a glimpse of a woman striding though the exhibits. His face lit up. "Hey Mom," he shouted, "we're over here." The woman turned, smiled, and headed their way.

"This is my Mom," said Joshua proudly. "She's one of the archaeologists here."

Danny's mouth gaped like a goldfish. It was the woman in the red jump suit, the one who had yelled at him.

"Hi, you must be Danny. I'm Mrs. Brokenhorn." Joshua's mother smiled. She didn't say anything about yelling, she just shook his hand. "Joshua's told me about you and I gather you have something you'd like to show me."

Danny nodded and fumbled in the pocket of his shorts. He handed her the somewhat grubby pile of tissues. Carefully, Mrs. Brokenhorn peeled them away until the lance point lay exposed on the palm of her hand.

"How lovely," she breathed. "Amazing it's still in one piece after all these years."

Danny and Joshua exchanged guilty grins. "More amazing than you know," thought Danny as he remembered rolling around on the ground after trying to lean on the wind.

"Danny, I think you have something really special

here," said Mrs. Brokenhorn. "Why don't you come to my office and we'll try to identify it."

Thrilled, Danny followed Mrs. Brokenhorn across the display area and through a door marked PRIVATE—STAFF ONLY.

"This is great. I've never met a real archaeologist before." Danny bubbled happily to Joshua. "Why didn't you tell me what your mother did?"

"You never asked," said Joshua with a grin.

"Idiot!" Danny stuck out a foot to trip Joshua up.

Joshua smartly jumped over it but stumbled against the corridor wall.

"You can't wrestle in here," warned his mother, opening a door and waving them inside. "There are too many things that could be broken."

Joshua saluted her saucily, but obediently went to sit quietly on the only empty chair. Danny hesitated in the doorway. The only other chair had a pile of books on it. He looked around in amazement. There were books everywhere. The walls were lined with them. Danny had never seen so many books except in the public library. Where there weren't books there were interesting objects, teeth and animal jawbones, lumps of rock, bones, pieces of pottery and several arrowheads. There was even a human skull among the papers on Mrs. Brokenhorn's desk.

Danny's eyes opened wide and he pointed wordlessly.

"That's a cast, you can handle it if you want to," said Mrs. Brokenhorn as she stepped past Danny, removed the books from the other chair and placed them on the floor.

Danny poked his finger in the skull's eye socket then pulled a face and perched on the edge of the cleared chair.

"Now, let's have a good look at this lance point." Mrs. Brokenhorn made a space on her desk and spread out a piece of blue paper. She angled a desk light so it shone on the paper and placed the lance point in the middle of the patch of light. The point gleamed and shone mystically.

Taking what looked like a long fine pair of steel tweezers, Mrs. Brokenhorn stretched them out so one steel tip gently touched each end of the point.

"What are you doing?" asked Danny curiously.

"I'm measuring. Using steel calipers is much more accurate than if I had tried to place the uneven surfaces of your lance point on a tape measure."

Danny and Joshua watched with fascination as Mrs. Brokenhorn used the calipers to measure not only the length, but the width and the depth on several places of the point. Then she took several photos of it. The last one she took with an instant print camera. "Here Danny," she said passing it over. "This one's for you."

The two boys hung over the photo and watched the picture magically develop before their eyes.

"Well," said Danny eagerly. "Is it something special? What kind of lance point is it?'

"I'm pretty sure it's a Scottsbluff point, and it's around 8000 years old," said Mrs. Brokenhorn, stroking the point gently.

Both boys whistled in admiration.

"If that's correct then it's pretty special," she continued, as she held it up to the light and they all admired it. "See how delicate it is. It's rare to find an undamaged lance point. It could have been made to use with an atlatl."

"An atal-whatl?" laughed Danny.

"An at-l-at-l." Mrs. Brokenhorn sounded out the syllables carefully so Danny could grasp the name. "It's a throwing stick to make a lance go further. Here!" she moved around the desk and picked up a pencil and paper. "I'll draw it to show you how it works."

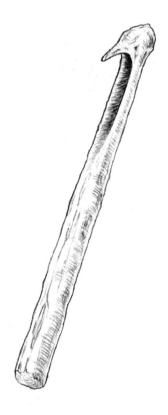

Danny gazed at her then down at the drawing. "I don't really get it," he said hesitantly.

Mrs. Brokenhorn smiled. "It seems pretty complicated, but all the atlatl really does is lengthen your arm so you can throw further. You could make one and see how it works."

"Really? Great, can we do it now?" Danny and Joshua bounced off their chairs eagerly.

"Hold on a second." Mrs. Brokenhorn suddenly turned serious. "There is something else I have to say."

Joshua sat back. He knew what was coming.

Danny sensed a change in the atmosphere, sat down again and looked warily from Joshua's mother to Joshua. "What's up?" he whispered.

"Just listen, but don't get mad," Joshua whispered back.

"Danny, did you know that archaeological finds are so important that they are protected by Alberta government laws?" asked Mrs. Brokenhorn.

"No," said Danny, "but that's good isn't it? Doesn't it stop people stealing things from your digs?"

"Yes," Mrs. Brokenhorn said, "but the law doesn't just protect digs. It covers any archaeological find in the province."

Danny looked at her puzzled. He sensed she was trying to tell him something but he wasn't sure what.

Mrs. Brokenhorn sighed. "Even archaeological finds as small as lance points, Danny." she said gently.

Danny stiffened with horror. "You mean... NO!" he yelled and grabbed the point off the desk and, clutching it protectively, thrust it deep in his pocket.

Why did everyone want his lance point? He'd found it, and it was special... Even before he knew it was 8000 years old, it was special. Besides... since he found the lucky lance point his dreams had been better. He didn't get chased by the 'Thing' anymore.

"You can't have it," his voice shook. "I found it so it's mine. You can't have it."

Joshua and his mother looked at each other then at Danny. But before Mrs. Brokenhorn could take a deep breath and explain, Danny slid off the chair, ran to the door and left.

Chapter Fifteen

Danny raced down the corridor, through the display area towards the elevators. He repeatedly pressed the call button, then found he couldn't bear to wait. He pushed blindly through a doorway marked STAIRS and rushed upwards. Legs pumping and chest heaving, he burst through an exit, into the fresh air.

He stood, gasping, at the top of the Buffalo Jump. It was empty. No visitors, no old man or Joshua. Just him, the landscape, the wind, and time to think.

Danny walked slowly along the edge of the jump.

The wind soothed and caressed him. It dried the sweat on his forehead and cooled his body. His lungs drew in grateful sage-sweet breaths and his heart gradually stopped thumping.

Danny sat down, his back against a sun-warmed rock, took the lance point out of his pocket and cupped it in the palm of his hands. It gleamed creamily and the orange threads through the chert sang in the sunshine. Danny drew a finger gently across the fluted edges and felt them nip and bite. "You're still sharp, even after 8000 years," he marvelled, "you could still do the job you were made for."

But what was the lance point's job now? It would never be used for hunting again. Should he keep it and use it to keep his fears at bay? It might get broken. Eight thousand years old, WOW! It was a miracle it had survived so long in his pocket. Should he give it to Mrs. Brokenhorn or to Joshua's grandfather? They were Peigans—maybe the point belonged to them. Danny felt guilty for taking something that he'd found on reserve land. Perhaps it should be in the Interpretive Centre. An 8000-year-old archaeological find should be looked after carefully. That was what museums and interpretive centres were for. But maybe he shouldn't have taken it in the first place. Maybe it belonged to the earth. The thoughts churned around and around in Danny's head and eventually crystallized into one big one. He was the finder and he loved and wanted the lance point, but who was its best keeper?

Danny looked down at the lance point. "You're beautiful," he whispered. "I wonder what the person who made you would want me to do." He clasped his hand tightly over the point, lay back against the rock, closed his eyes and tried to visualize the original maker.

The young man with one eagle feather in his headband was checking the binding on his new lance. It was a good lance. The unusual cream chert had been difficult to knap but it made a fine sharp point. The sinews binding the point in place had dried strongly and tightly and the lance shaft ran straight and true. It was almost ready to use. He flexed his arm and tried out a throw. The lance sped swiftly upwards then curved back to earth to embed itself in some soft prairie. It had flown well but not as far as the young man would like. The young man sighed. His arm was still not as strong or as powerful as some of the older hunters'. No matter how many hours he exercised and practiced, he could not throw as fast or as far as White Calf or Running Wolf. Still an atlatl would help. He would craft a special one to match his lance.

Picking up his lance, the hunter strode across the prairie and down into a small coulee to search for suitable wood. He walked down towards the river, passing several bushes of juniper. He ignored them. Juniper stems were twisted and gnarled, he wanted a cottonwood tree. One with the wood grain running straight through the length of the branch.

With the same patience that he had knapped the point, the young man searched for the right piece of wood. He knew he would find it if he looked long enough and in the right places. There it was, a light but sturdy branch on a young cottonwood tree overhanging the Oldman River. It had side branches running off in the right place to make a notch for the lance. He pulled out his obsidian knife and chipped it off.

The young man sat on the riverbank and trimmed off one side shoot from the branch and peeled and smoothed the wood, checking it against his lance. Then came the hard part. Patiently the young man trimmed the remaining side shoot to leave a small spur, then pared and scraped a shallow groove along the top of the branch until it met the spur forming a little hollow. It took time, for he wanted the groove smooth and even with no bumps or nicks. Eventually he ran his fingers delicately over the wood and smiled with satisfaction. It was smooth. He had made an atlatl. He picked up the atlatl and lance and eagerly ran up the coulee, to try them out on the prairie.

The young hunter paused and looked around at the empty landscape. He was several miles from his tribe's summer camp and had this patch of prairie to himself. He had purposely come far so no one would see if his attempts at making a lance and atlatl failed.

The hunter placed the lance snugly in the groove across the top edge of the atlatl, the end tucked up to the spur. He curled his first finger over the top of the lance to keep it steady and held the bottom of the atlatl firmly with his thumbs and the remaining three fingers of his right hand. He lifted them shoulder high for a few seconds, to feel the balance. It wasn't right. The stone point made the lance head too heavy to sit easily on the length of the atlatl. He needed something on the atlatl to balance the weight.

The hunter lowered his arm and looked around. There was a long narrow pebble. That might work. Using some spare sinew from his pouch the young man bound the pebble towards the back length of the atlatl, then laid the lance shaft in place again. It took several tries before he placed the counterweight correctly, but finally, when he held the lance and atlatl up in the strike position, they balanced perfectly. Patiently he cut two grooves for the pebble's binding so that the lance would still fit smoothly on top of it. It was time to try again.

Holding lance and atlatl at shoulder height, the young hunter started to run, his long legs pounding across the prairie. He drew his arm back as he gained momentum and with as much strength as he could, threw towards the sun. The atlatl powerfully thrust the lance forward. Swiftly it sped skyward, higher and higher in a big beautiful curve. With a great cry of triumph the young man spread his arms. It was a good throw, almost equal to the best that White Calf could do.

It was the cry that startled Danny. His eyes flew open and he sat up suddenly. The cry came again, and a shadow passed over Danny's body. He squinted against the sun and saw not the young man with the eagle feather and dream lance, but a Bald Eagle.

"Young men have to earn eagle feathers," echoed the Old Man's voice in Danny's head. "Your time will come."

Danny stood up and squared his shoulders.

Remembering the patience and persistence of the young hunter and the strength and courage of the eagle, Danny walked determinedly back to the Interpretive Centre and called the elevator.

He stepped out on the display level, and walked through the PRIVATE door, down the corridor to Mrs. Brokenhorn's office. He paused, took a deep breath, rapped firmly on the door, and cautiously opened it.

Joshua and his mother were still there, talking quietly. Joshua's face lit up when he saw Danny but he said nothing, just watched as Danny came into the office.

Danny hesitated then walked slowly over to the desk.

Mrs. Brokenhorn smiled and waited for him to speak.

"I'm sorry I got mad. I know my point's important, but I need it for my school project... and I need time... I can't figure it out. I don't know if the lance point should be here, or maybe I should give it to Joshua's grandfather. I'm not sure who it really belongs to."

"I'm not really sure, either Danny," Mrs. Brokenhorn admitted softly.

Danny looked at her in surprise."You're not?"

Mrs. Brokenhorn pushed her dark hair back from her forehead and leaned back thoughtfully. "No, you see, the person who made this lance point may not have been Peigan. We don't know what nations used the Jump in the early days. So even if you thought the lance point should be given back to the people of the First Nations, no one would know which group to give it to."

Danny felt a small measure of relief. "So I'm not the only one trying to figure it out?"

Mrs. Brokenhorn smiled, stood up and walked around the desk. She patted Danny on the shoulder.

"No, this is something I deal with all the time. Joshua has told me how important this point is to you, but I want you to seriously think about it and its place in history. I'm not going to insist you donate it to the museum now.... no one is going to snatch it from you... I'm going to trust that you think it through and do the right thing."

She looked across at Joshua. "So, are you going to take Danny to the pow wow?"

"The drums... I'd forgotten," said Danny, "Will I get to see the drummers?"

"You bet," said Joshua. "And the dancers. Let's go."

Chapter Sixteen

Joshua and Danny ran exuberantly down the hill. The drumming had stopped but news of the pow wow had spread around the Interpretive Centre and other visitors streamed and flowed through the tipi ring towards the arbour of branches. Danny followed Joshua closely and they wove expertly through the crowd and dodged under an leafy archway into the dancing ground.

Danny caught his breath in awe. The dancing ground was large, a gym-sized patch of prairie grass covered with long strips of carpet. "The carpet keeps the dust down when we're dancing," explained Joshua.

All along one side, under the shade of the arbour sat the drum teams. Danny counted eleven drums. No wonder he had heard the drumming all the way up the hill. The drums were large, mounted on stands decorated with bright streamers and feathers. Each drumming and singing team sat in a group around their drum. The team members were dressed in traditional clothes, most were men, some wearing white stetsons to keep the sun off their faces, but some drums had several women as team members. The size of the teams varied. Some drums had three or four people sitting around them, others as many as twelve members each with their own drumsticks at the ready.

"It's awesome," breathed Danny as he looked at the gaily decorated drums and spectacularly clothed teams.

"You wait," replied Joshua. "The dancers will be in soon." He pointed to a main entrance at the far end of the dancing ground. Danny could see many traditionally costumed people milling around. "Everyone's assembling for the grand entrance," said Joshua hurriedly, "I have to go and join them. You can sit on any seat on this side of the dancing ground." He waved his hand briefly towards the arbour wall behind Danny. "I'll be back after the procession." Joshua ran lightly across the strips of carpet and vanished into the colourful crowd thronging the entrance.

Feeling abandoned, Danny looked around. There were plenty of empty benches, sheltered from the sun by the leafy bower. He chose a middle one, grateful it was in the shade, for the afternoon sun was beating down fiercely. No one joined him. The drum teams were poised on the far side of the ground, and all the First Nations people seemed to be outside the main entrance waiting for something. The other white visitors were dotted in small groups around the empty benches. They looked as uncomfortable as Danny felt, squatting uneasily on their strip of bench, ignoring each other's presence and obviously wondering what they had let themselves in for.

Then, at a hidden signal the drumming started and a disembodied voice spoke from the loud speaker. "Will you please rise for the grand entrance."

Danny scrambled to his feet.

Slowly and solemnly a great procession entered the dancing grounds and wound around. First came a young man proudly carrying a tall banner made of many eagle feathers. He was followed by three flag bearers wearing the long flowing feathered ceremonial head-dresses. Danny recognized two of the flags, the Canadian maple leaf and Alberta's provincial flag. The third flag he had not seen before, it was brilliant red with a white circle in the middle containing a large black buffalo. Eagle feathers radiated from the bottom of the circle.

Then came the elders. They entered six abreast in several lines. They walked slowly and rhythmically with a tiny pause between each step, following the insistent beat of the drums. Danny recognized Joshua's grandfather in the first row and he grinned hugely, but the old man was intent and stared straight ahead, solemnly leading his people around the dancing ground. Then the rest of the dancers moved in, again six abreast. Slowly the space became a dazzling array of colour. The sun shone and sparkled from a million beads sewn into elaborate patterns. Men, women, and children filed past dressed in buckskin, moosehide, flowing jewel-colored shawls, and a multitude of incredible headdresses. They carried eagle feather fans, blankets folded over their arms, elaborately painted skin shields or beaded pouches. They wheeled gracefully around and around until the last set of dancers had entered. The dancing ground was full of a slow, stately whirling kaleidoscope of vivid colour and beauty. Nothing Danny had ever seen or read had prepared him for this sight. It was magnificent.

The drumming stopped, and everyone silently faced the same way. Danny craned his neck trying to see Joshua, but there were far to many people in too many costumes to be able to pick him out. An important looking man in white-beaded deerskin with flowing fringes and flowing headdress stepped from the first row, closely followed by Joshua's grandfather. Together they walked up to a microphone.

Once again it was obvious that the Old Man was offering up a prayer in Blackfoot. Danny shut his eyes tight and listened to the music of the language.

"Weird," thought Danny. "I'm only a few miles from home but it's a different world with a different language. I wonder if this is how Joshua's people feel when they visit Fort Macleod."

Once the prayer and the greetings had finished, the atmosphere changed. Smiling and talking quietly amongst themselves, the crowd dispersed from the centre space and filled up the benches. Danny found himself sharing his bench with an extended family of parents, children, cousins, uncles, and aunts. He exchanged shy smiles with them and waited to see what would happen next.

One of the drum teams commenced drumming and singing. Slowly people rose, formed a circle and began a dance. Danny watched as Joshua and a couple of friends stomped and jigged past. Joshua grinned and Danny waved. The dance was a long one and the beat hypnotic. Danny relaxed and lost himself in the swirl of colour and pageantry.

"Hey, you hungry?" A grinning Joshua reappeared and interrupted his thoughts by thrusting a large pizza-sized object under his nose.

"What is it?" asked Danny doubtfully. It smelled good but looked weird. Like pizza crust that had risen and bubbled too much. It was covered with something that glistened and dripped.

"Fried bannock with butter and honey," said Joshua tearing it in half and thrusting some into Danny hands. "Try it. It's good."

Tentatively Danny took a tiny nibble. "Mmm," he mumbled enthusiastically and took a great bite, licking his lips as the hot honey and butter dribbled down his chin. "Great but messy," he laughed in between chews.

Companionably the boys watched the dancing. Competitions for the best male dancers, female dancers, and costumes were held in between communal grass dances in which all the First Nations people left their benches and joined in together. Danny watched intently. His feet tapped to the insistent rhythm of the drums. He almost wished he could dance. He intently watched the feet of the dancers as they shuffled past. The basic step seemed easy enough if his body would just catch the rhythm, but the elaborate footwork done during the dance competitions took his breath away.

As if someone had been mind reading, an announcement came over the loudspeaker. It was the chief.

"We have several visitors at our pow wow today. We

would like to invite them to join in a Friendship Dance."

"Come on Danny, that means you." Joshua leaped up and tried to drag Danny with him.

Danny hung back. "I can't," he mumbled, embarrassed. "I'm a real klutz."

Joshua looked at Danny. "My people don't often invite visitors to join in," he said seriously. "This is a friendship dance."

Danny flushed with embarrassment. "I can't," he insisted, scared of making a fool of himself. "I can't dance to save my life, I'm no good at gym or anything like that." He hesitated. "I'll trip over my feet and everyone will laugh," he finished honestly.

Joshua stuck out a hand and heaved Danny off the bench. "I've already told you... this is a friendship dance, we don't laugh at our friends."

Joshua dragged a reluctant Danny onto the dancing ground amongst a group of young boys. They said something in Blackfoot to Joshua and he laughingly replied, then turned to Danny. "Right Danny, let's see how fast you can catch on. Watch us and we'll help you with the basic step, but once you've got that... watch out!"

"OK," said Danny resignedly. "But don't blame me if your friends all die laughing."

The drums started and everyone's feet responded, even Danny's.

Stomp tap, Stomp tap, Stomp tap, Stomp tap....

It took a while but surrounded by Joshua's friends encouraging him, Danny slowly managed to catch on to the the basic step.

Stomp tap, Stomp tap, Stomp tap, Stomp tap....

It came a little easier. Danny concentrated as the dancers, First Nations and white, pounded rhythmically around in a large circle.

"This is harder than it looks," Danny gasped to Joshua as his calf muscles clenched and cramped in protest.

"Hang in," encouraged Joshua, "feel the beat."

Danny gained confidence and started to relax, not just

listening with his ears but feeling the rhythm from the drums and making his body part of the drumbeat.

"Hey man, you've got it," laughed Joshua and Danny grinned, lost the beat then caught it again.

Stomp tap, Stomp tap, stomp tap, Stomp tap.

"I am getting it, I'm really getting it," realized Danny triumphantly. He began to enjoy himself.

"Now," said Joshua from behind him. "Let's try some fancy bits."

Suddenly Danny was surrounded by young men dancing up a storm. Tiny puffs of dust arose from their stomping feet even through the strips of carpet. The drums pounded and the arbour branches shivered and shook in reply. Moccasined toes made elaborated patterns and bodies wove around and around. The drumming intensified and the singing rose high above it.

"Come on Danny," yelled Joshua over the drums. "Dance!"

And Danny danced. His legs bent and he strutted like the Prairie Chicken. His arms crooked and became wings, his feet pounded the earth and became part of its heartbeat. Danny danced till his body ached and the sweat poured down his head and back. He danced till the dust rose and the sky whirled. Danny danced till he could dance no more.

"Not bad for a whitey," said one of Joshua's friends as Danny staggered breathlessly back to his seat as the drums finally ceased. "Not bad at all."

Danny collapsed onto the bench, panting.

The pow wow continued through the hot afternoon, and by sunset showed no sign of abating.

"I have to go," said Danny reluctantly. "My mom will be here soon." He looked curiously at Joshua. "When does it finish?"

Joshua shrugged. "Some folks will dance and drum all night," he said. "But dancers in the finals tomorrow will go to bed early." He yawned. "I'll walk up to the car park with you."

The two boys toiled up the hill and stood on the low

concrete edging. The drumming was faint now, but still insistently pulsing through the evening air. They watched for the car.

"Next week," said Danny hesitantly, "could you come over to my place?"

"Guess so," said Joshua. "Will your folks mind?"

"No. They like me having friends over."

"Even friends from the reserve?'

"Idiot," said Danny, tickling Joshua till he wobbled off the concrete ledge. And they chased each other around the car park until Danny's mom arrived and Joshua waved him off.

Chapter Seventeen

Humming happily under his breath, Danny bent over the kitchen table and concentrated on the piece of wood in front of him. It was an off-cut of light balsa wood that looked big enough to make a replacement blade for Brett Gibson's helicopter. Danny placed both pieces of the broken rotor blade carefully on top of the balsa and traced around the edges with a pencil. Yes, they fitted. If he cut and shaped carefully, his idea should work. Danny opened his tool box and got out his equipment. He lined everything up in front of him, his razor-sharp knife, sandpaper, pencil, ruler and a cutting board. He loved weekends at home. Time to do things he was good at, no school, and no one yelling if he worked slowly. He wished the whole week could be made up of weekends.

Actually, the week at school since the pow wow had been surprisingly bearable. Danny was puzzled though that he'd not heard from Carol; she'd promised to get in touch with him, but perhaps she was busy. Apart from that, the only other irritation had been Brett Gibson's bugging.

"You fixed my helicopter yet, Dummy?" had been Brett's daily greeting on the school bus.

Danny sighed. Brett had a point. Danny really should

have fixed the helicopter last weekend, but going to the pow wow and working on his project outline had taken up all his time.

Tapping his pencil thoughtfully against his teeth, Danny reviewed the past week, wondering what had made the difference. "Must be my lucky lance point," he thought. "Mr. Berg hardly got mad at me at all."

Mr. Berg had raised his eyebrows when Danny handed in a typewritten project outline.

"It's all my work, honest, Mr. Berg." Danny had quickly explained. "My mom just typed it so you could read it."

Mr. Berg had grunted but accepted the work. In fact Mr. Berg only lost his temper with Danny once that week. Danny grinned as he remembered the incident. It had been a blast.

Danny and Mike had been shoving each other trying to be first to get a drink from the water fountain after gym. The combined weight of the two boys wrestling on the edge of the ancient basin pulled the whole unit away from the wall. The plaster flaked away at the back, the pipe broke and cold water spewed out across the corridor. Danny and Michael were instantly soaked, but laughing so hard and hysterically that they couldn't call for help. The water poured out in a huge fountain and formed a lake at their feet. Both boys, helpless and hiccupping with laughter, tried to catch their breath enough to shout. They needn't have bothered. Guess who did it for them?

"Hey Mr. Berg!" Brett Gibson yelled as he came out of the gym and saw what was happening. "Dummy Danny's trying to flood the school."

Half the class rushed out excitedly to paddle in the corridor. Marylise tried to stop the water by stuffing her fist in the top of the broken pipe, but the force of the water made three jets instead of one, soaking some of the bystanders.

"Surf's up," hollered Brett Gibson and took a running dive through the water and slid on his belly over the wet linoleum, down the length of the corridor. Several other kids promptly followed.

Mr. Berg erupted angrily from the gym, roared at them, then raced off down into the basement to find the janitor and the stop tap.

By the time the water had been turned off the entire Grade 5 class was drenched to the skin and Mr. Berg had furiously given them all a detention. They had to change back into gym shorts and spread their clothes out on the playing field to dry in the sunshine. The class was lectured for behaving like kindergarten kids and Michael and Danny spent the rest of the morning helping the janitor mop up.

Danny chuckled out loud; he'd missed math and science during clean up, and all the class seemed to think the riot was worth a DT. He'd even glimpsed Mr. Berg laughing as he explained the uproar to the staff. Not a bad deal all round.

"You sound in a good mood, son." Danny's father entered the kitchen, poured a cup of coffee from the coffee pot and sat at the table. "What are you up to today?"

Danny pushed the helicopter over to his father. "I'm making a new rotor blade for this."

His father picked up the helicopter and the broken blade and examined them. "This the one you broke? Brett Gibson's?" he asked.

Danny flushed. "How did you know?"

His father grinned. "It's a small town, son. You learn a lot in a store just by keeping your ears open." He put down the helicopter and nodded towards the wood in front of Danny. "Think you can do it?"

"I think so," said Danny slowly. "The shape's easy enough, and if I sand down the outer edges of the blade it will give the right angle. I'll paint the wood white. It should look OK if I give it several coats."

His father patted Danny's shoulder. "Sounds good to me. Ask if you run into trouble attaching it. I'll be around later, but I've got to go over to MacVeys to help with their new bull." He drained his coffee and got up to leave.

"Oh Dad," Danny said hesitantly, "I wanted to ask you something... it's about the museum. Are you still on the museum board?"

"Sure, been on for years. I don't go to all the meetings though. A lot of yattering and no action. Why?"

Danny sat marshalling his thoughts for a minute. This was a tricky one. He had waited all week for a good time to tackle his dad, but Danny wasn't altogether sure his father would understand.

"Well," Danny chose his words carefully. "You know about this First Nations project I'm researching?"

His father nodded.

"We'll, I've found something out. Something they should know about one of the exhibits. It shouldn't be there."

Danny's father came and sat down at the kitchen table again. "Hmm. Sounds tricky. You sure you know what you're talking about?"

Danny nodded.

"This something to do with the Indian kid you hang around with?"

Danny looked uncomfortable. "Well, kind of, but not really. It's something he first told me about, but it's not really anything to do with Joshua."

Mr. Budzynski sighed, folded his arms and stretched out his legs. "OK, spit it out. I guess I'd better hear the whole story."

Danny gave his father a carefully edited version of the Elders' view of the photo of the Sundance. He stumbled a few times trying to keep his story straight because he didn't want to mention the illicit visit to the museum where Joshua first saw the photograph.

"You mean you've got yourself into a snit over a photo?" Danny's father said unbelievingly. "No one's going to take that seriously."

"But they've got to, Dad. It's real important to the Peigans. The Sundance is sacred, it's holy. The photo shouldn't be there."

"Look, son if those Indians are putting pressure on you, I'm going to have a thing or two to say to them."

"No," cried Danny. "It's not like that. No one said anything... They wouldn't... but I care." He looked desperately across at his father, willing him to understand. "Come on, Dad. You're always telling me 'Be a man, stand up for something you believe in.' Well I've found out something. And it's wrong. And I'm the only one that knows. So I have to say something, don't I?"

There was a long silence while Danny looked at his father.

Mr. Budzynski shifted uncomfortably in his chair. "Look, this is a tough one, son. It lands me in a spot. Let me think about it." Danny's father stood up. "I'll take a look at that photo and see what I can find out about it at the next meeting. OK?"

Danny smiled, relieved that his father hadn't poured too much cold water on his idea.

Mr. Budzynski pulled on his sweater and headed for the door. He paused at the door and looked back at Danny. "I know you and I don't always get on about your math, son," he said. "But you've got a good heart, I'll give you that."

Danny bent happily over his work. Praise from his dad was rare.

Chapter Eighteen

"Every day's been a good one for ages," thought Danny happily as he stretched lazily in bed, enjoying the Sunday morning feeling of waking without the alarm. He rolled over and looked at his dresser. Brett's helicopter was still there, looking almost as good as new.

The helicopter gleamed in a patch of daylight streaming in from where his curtains didn't quite meet in the centre. From a distance the new rotor blade looked almost identical to the old one. Danny leaned over and touched it with one finger. The layers of fast drying acrylic paint had made a tough shiny white finish. Danny flicked the blade and watched carefully as it spun around evenly and smoothly. He had managed to fix it himself except for the rivet holding it on. His dad had done that for him.

"That should shut up Brett Gibson for a while," Danny said in a satisfied tone of voice. "I'll give it to him on Monday." He turned his head and squinted at his clock.

"Nine o'clock! Holy cow, Joshua will be here soon." He swung his legs out of bed and started hunting in the mess on the floor for some clothes.

In fact it was after ten before Joshua arrived. Danny was in the back yard throwing some feed down for the hens when he heard a truck pull up and Ringo's frantic barks. He dumped the bucket and ran down the farm track to the gate.

"Hello big puppy," Joshua was saying as he bent over and rubbed Ringo's ears. "Some fierce watch dog you are."

Ringo, ecstatic at having another boy to play with, stopped barking and rolled over on his back, paws flopping in the air and tongue lolling out to the side.

"Stupid mutt," said Danny fondly as he joined Joshua in rubbing Ringo's belly. Ringo's long tongue swept Danny's face and his tail frantically stirred the dust. "You're supposed to scare strangers, not invite them to scratch your belly."

"Fat chance," laughed Joshua. "You should have trained him to hate people, not like people."

Danny sat back on his haunches. "Do you?"

"Do I what?"

"Do you like people?"

Joshua paused rubbing and considered. "Depends. Not that many white people. What about you?"

Danny chuckled. "Not that many white people either."

Both boys laughed and Ringo wriggled from under their hands and stood upright, barking excitedly.

Danny jumped to his feet, took Ringo's head in his hands and looked deep into his eyes. "Hey Ringo! Shall we trust Joshua? Shall we show Joshua our secret place?"

The dog barked and wagged its tail furiously.

"Go on then, boy. Let's have an adventure. Ringo, show us the den!"

Ringo turned and trotted across the fields.

"Follow that dog," shouted Danny, and both boys ran.

✿

"Hey man, this is really something." Joshua wriggled through the opening in the coulee wall and delightedly surveyed Danny's den.

Danny showed him the pickle jar lanterns and even

though it was morning they lit one and entered the branch tipi. Ringo followed them through the doorway and flopped down between their feet and the log table.

Joshua fished in his pocket and brought out an envelope. "Here, Mom sent you this."

Danny ripped it open and lifted out a folded piece of paper. It was a copy of a donor certificate, explaining how an object could be given to the Interpretive Centre. Danny read it carefully then refolded and placed it back in the envelope. "Tell your mom thanks," he said quietly as he tucked it in his pocket. "I've not forgotten what she said. I'm keeping the point safe. Actually I've been trying to copy it." He fiddled behind the log table and brought out his rag bundle, unwrapped it and held out the rocky shards to Joshua.

Joshua carefully cradled the points in his hand. "You made these?"

"Yes. They're not very good though," said Danny. "I'm still practicing."

"I think they're great. It's hard to knap points. You've got several really good ones here."

Danny looked carefully at the worked stones then delicately picked one out. "Here."

"You giving me one?'

"Yup. I thought if we each had one we could try and make a lance and an atlatl."

"Great," said Joshua wrapping the point carefully in a tissue. "We'll need sticks and pocket knives, have you got one?" He felt in his pocket and pulled out a small scout knife.

Danny pulled out a similar knife. "We'll have to do it outside though. There's not enough room in here. The lances need to be pretty long. Come and look, I found some great willow branches."

The boys crawled out into the gully and Danny passed over some willow sticks he'd already cut. They sat whittling for a long time.

"This is hard," grumbled Joshua after his third failure at binding the point onto the lance with fishing line.

"I know, the line is slippery. We're supposed to use sinew but I don't know where to get it or how to make it. Would your Mom know?"

"I'll ask." Joshua stood up. "This is the best I can do. Come on. Let's throw them."

Danny eyed the lances and atlatls doubtfully. "I think they need more work... besides I think we need to glue flight feathers on the lance shafts." He lifted up his lance and looked down its length. "Mine's not very straight."

"Aw come on. You're such a perfectionist, let's just throw them anyway."

They climbed to the top of the coulee and stood side by side, lances poised. Ringo waited, tail wafting slowly.

"Hey... I'm a mighty hunter," said Danny proudly. He held his lance at shoulder height. "Let's aim for that sage bush." He pointed to a clump about 10 metres away. "On the count of three. One... two... THREE."

Two lances thudded to the ground hardly a length away. Ringo barked excitedly.

"Huh," snorted Joshua in disgust as he retrieved them. "Fine hunters we'd be. Wonder if the atlatl will make a difference." They picked up the spurred sticks they had whittled and tried to balance the lance shafts on the atlatls with only a couple of fingers.

"One ... two... THREE," counted Danny.

Once more the lances thudded to the ground a couple of metres away.

"Shoot," said Danny in frustration. "My point has come off."

"Guess we haven't made them properly," sighed Joshua "Now what?"

"We try again," said Danny and they headed back to the den.

☼

"I talked to my Dad this morning," Danny said as he put his knife down and stretched his cramped fingers. "He's on the museum board. I'm going to ask the museum to take down the Sundance photograph."

Joshua's eyes widened. "Think they will?"

Danny shrugged. "Dunno."

"What if they won't listen to you?"

Danny shrugged again. "Dunno. Guess I'll have to think of something else."

"Like what?"

"Well... I could sneak in and take it."

"You can't do that," said Joshua shocked to the core. "That's stealing a museum artifact."

"Hey, I thought you said it shouldn't be there," said Danny, hurt. "I thought you'd be pleased I was trying to do something about it."

"I am, I am." Joshua argued. "But there would be one heck of a lot of trouble if we broke into the museum and stole something. The reserve would have the whole town on its neck."

"What's all this 'we'," said Danny. "I'm not asking you to do anything."

"I know," said Joshua softly. "But we're friends aren't we? I told you about it, so I guess we're in this together. OK?"

"You mean... you'd come too?" said Danny unbelievingly.

Joshua nodded. "Sure. If that was the only way."

"That would be great, really great," bubbled Danny, then he sobered up and looked solemn. "But wouldn't you be a bit scared?"

Joshua thought for a moment. "A bit," he admitted. "We might be smarter to see if your Dad could do something first. Maybe he could get us in to meet with the board so we could explain."

Danny stood up and stretched. "That's a good idea. Let's go and ask him. He'll be in the store."

✿

It didn't take the boys long to get into town. No sooner had they started walking down the highway than Mr. MacVey's truck came barrelling along and he offered them a lift.

"Uh oh," said Danny as they leapt out on Main street, opposite the store. "The tourist season's started."

Joshua looked down the street and saw several tour buses on the museum parking lot. "So what?" he asked, puzzled.

"That's when Dad wants me to help out in the store. I hate it," muttered Danny. "Maybe I shouldn't show my face in there today."

"Aw come on. I haven't seen inside your store, we usually shop at the big supermarket at the other end of town."

Reluctantly Danny pushed open the door of the small general store and the boys stepped inside.

It was an old store, one of the original buildings in Fort Macleod, and Mr. Budzynski had tried to keep the old-fashioned feel that the tourists enjoyed. The dark wood shelves were stocked with all kinds of food staples, but fishing rods and nets hung from hooks in the ceiling, gold pans spilled out from one corner, art and stationery supplies, camping supplies, postcards and souvenirs all jostled for room along the back wall. Mr. Budzynski had also improved the store's popularity with both tourists and town folk by squeezing in a Fifties-style ice cream bar with 42 different flavours to choose from.

Today the place was packed with people. Several older people from the tour bus, sporting plastic daisies in their lapels proclaiming, 'HI I'm a Sunday Sightseeing Senior' poked around in the souvenir section, and a bunch of families lined up patiently for ice cream.

"Thank goodness you're here, Danny. I'm short-handed. Could you handle the ice cream bar and cash register, while I work at the grocery cash register?" Mr. Budzynski, sweating and harried, tried to deal quickly with the line-up of customers as well as rushing to the other side of the store to serve ice cream.

Danny groaned. "Told you we shouldn't have come in," he muttered to Joshua. "Where's Ginny Taber?" he asked his father.

His father shrugged. "She didn't turn up again. Come on Danny, there are customers waiting."

"Dad, I'm no good on the cash register. Can't I do something else?"

"Danny, for once just shut up, concentrate, and help me out."

Danny seemed to shrink in on himself but obediently turned, slipped between the customers and headed to the ice cream bar. Joshua followed and ducked behind the counter with him.

"Hey, I'm good at math," Joshua whispered, eyes dancing. "I'll work the till if you show me how, and you can do the ice creams."

Danny looked at him, hope dawning. "You will? You don't mind?"

"I love doing jobs like this," said Joshua happily. "Just show me how it works and tell me how much the ice creams are."

It took Joshua all of two seconds to catch on to the workings of the electronic till.

"The ice creams are fifty cents a scoop," Danny whispered as he rapidly tied on an apron and picked up the metal scoop, "so the cost goes by how many scoops they want, then the till works out the tax."

"That's easy enough," said Joshua as he looked at the first customer. "Can I help you?" he asked with a grin.

Danny scooped and scooped, till his back ached and his hand was numb from being in the freezer all the time. The hot afternoon ensured a steady stream of customers all wanting different combinations.

"A double of chocolate and amaretto..."

"A triple with vanilla, orange, and bubblegum..."

"Two triples and a quad. Rocky road, tiger, smartie and strawberry, for the quad; one triple with choc chip, mint and Irish cream; the other with tangerine, double chocolate and cheesecake."

The orders grew more and more fantastic as the day wore on.

Joshua, with eyes sparkling and a ready chuckle, was in his element. He could calculate how much the customer owed before he'd rung up the order, he never fumbled with the change, and he always had a joke for the folks in the line-up.

Danny, much to his surprise, also enjoyed himself. He didn't mind scooping ice cream as long as he didn't have to figure out the money. Danny knew all 42 flavours and their whereabouts in the freezer. He had a great knack of slapping the triple scoops on just right so they didn't fall off (at least not until the customer was some way down the road). The ice cream line had never moved so fast or so smoothly and the contented customers left, licking their cones.

"You two are quite the team." Mr. Budzynski stood in front of them. He stuck out a hand across the counter. "You must be Joshua. Good to meet you. Nice of you to pitch in."

"It was fun," said Joshua, shaking his hand.

Mr. Budzynski walked over to the door, put up the CLOSED sign and drew down the blind. "We close early on a Sunday," he said, "so you're off the hook now. Help yourselves to an ice cream and I'll see you later with your wages."

"Wages?" said Joshua unbelievingly. "You mean we get paid? I thought we were just doing it to help out."

"I pay my staff, so I pay Danny when he helps out. Only minimum wage though, so don't get excited." Mr. Budzynski laughed.

Joshua turned to Danny. "You mean you hate working in the store so much that you don't want to do it even though you get paid?"

Danny nodded, not looking at his father.

"You're crazy, I'd do it." Joshua looked hesitantly at Mr. Budzynski. "If Danny really doesn't want the job.... Is it possible Mr. Budzynski? Could I have Danny's job?"

"Well, it's not a real job," Mr. Budzynski hedged. "Danny doesn't work all the time, he's not old enough. Neither are you. I just like him to help out on Sunday afternoons in the summer."

"Wasn't I good enough?" asked Joshua, downcast. "I thought we did alright."

Mr. Budzynski patted his shoulder. "You did a great job, you were really quick on the till."

"Joshua's good at math," said Danny, proud of his friend.

Mr. Budzynski looked strangely at his son. "You really do hate working in the store, don't you Danny?"

Danny flushed and nodded. "I'm no good at it Dad. I mess up the money. Today was only OK because Joshua worked the till."

Mr. Budzynski looked thoughtfully at Joshua again. "Joshua, I don't know you very well. This is the first time we've met, but I like what I see."

Joshua said nothing, just looked at him eagerly.

Mr. Budzynski laughed. "Look, it's not a proper job, but if your Mom will give written permission, I'll try you out on the ice cream bar for three hours next Sunday. If you and I still get along, you've got yourself a regular spot on Sundays."

"YIPEEE!" Joshua grabbed Danny and they jigged around the counter.

Danny broke away and came over and hugged his dad. "So I never have to work the cash again, Dad?"

His father looked down at him, a strange expression on his face. "If you really hate it that much, I guess not, son," he said slowly.

"WHEEW..." Danny expelled a sigh of relief as though the weight of the world had tumbled from his shoulders. "Thanks Dad." He gave his father a brilliant smile and another hug before he and Joshua rushed off happily to eat their ice creams outside, all other problems forgotten.

Sadly, Mr. Budzynski watched them through the store window, then blew his nose hard and carried on locking up the store.

Chapter Nineteen

Danny sat on the floor of his bedroom and ran his hand lovingly up and down the shaft of his finished lance. Maybe Joshua was right, he was a perfectionist. He'd certainly not been able to rest until he'd practiced and found out how to throw the lance and atlatl properly. He'd also worked for hours to make them look beautiful.

Balancing the lance across his fingers, Danny felt a warm glow of pleasure and pride. Red chicken feathers had made good strong "fletching" at the end of the lance. He'd painstakingly tried the fletching several times, first with two, then with three and finally four feathers, but three seemed to work the best so that's what he'd settled on. Then he'd finally solved the problem of attaching the stone point by using waxed dental floss instead of fishing line, and so far it seemed to be holding. He laid the lance gently on the floor and picked up the atlatl.

Yes, that felt right too. Danny had whittled, smoothed, and rubbed it with fine sandpaper, then finally polished it with wax. The peeled wood gleamed with a greenish cast and it felt good to the touch. Last night he'd found a long narrow pebble to use as a counterweight and carefully scraped a groove around it with one of his dad's tools. Now he was able to bind it on to the atlatl where he'd cut a matching groove in the wood so that the cord wouldn't stop the smooth seating of the lance.

Danny stretched and looked at his watch. It was only 10 minutes after seven. There was still time to practice his throwing before the sun set.

"Mom, I'm just going out to the cow pasture. I won't be long," Danny called as he passed the living room where his folks were watching TV.

A chilly breeze made him shiver as he stepped out of the house but he couldn't be bothered going back for a jacket. He climbed over the fence into the cow pasture and stood poised with the lance and atlatl at shoulder height. The breeze blew stronger and he felt goose pimples rise on his arms.

It was winter and the tribe, starving and ill, huddled together in one tipi for warmth. The only member with any strength left was the young hunter Danny Three Feathers. "You are the only one who can save us," said the chief. "Take your lance and atlatl and find us some food." Three Feathers headed out onto the frozen prairie, lance poised ready and eyes watchful. He walked for miles and miles but saw nothing, not even a jack rabbit.

By the end of the day Three Feathers was exhausted and discouraged. He had found nothing to eat other than a few berries. The light was fading but he knew he could not return to the tipi without food so he stopped, faced into the freezing wind, visualized a buffalo in his mind and called upon the Great Spirit.

"Please save my people, they are starving. Help us by sending some game so I will not go back empty-handed." He prayed for a long time and then sang what he could remember of the Holy Woman's song. The Great Spirit answered his prayer. Three Feathers heard the distant drumming of hooves, then smelled the musty sweat of the great beast and heard it snort.

Danny, completely wrapped up in his daydream, stealthily crept across the cow pasture towards the buffalo-shaped dogwood bushes on the far side. Holding the lance and atlatl steady, he began to run, faster and faster... NOW. He let go and the lance shot forward and sailed over the top of the dogwoods in a perfect arc while the atlatl dropped to his feet.

"WOW," he breathed in triumph.

An enormous bellow shook the evening and a dark shape came charging through the dogwoods, head down and feet pounding.

"Holy cow, I got a real buffalo... and it's real mad." Terrified, Danny took to his heels and headed towards the fence.

The angry animal pounded closer and closer. Danny could hear it fiercely snorting and imagined he was feeling its fetid breath on his neck. Panic-stricken, he redoubled his efforts, pumping his legs so fast he was almost flying. His fingers barely touched the fence as he vaulted over and collapsed in a heap on the other side.

"Danny, are you OK out there?" called his dad through the kitchen window.

"Er, yes," Danny called back shakily.

"I forgot to warn you, Mr. McVey's young bull is in the pasture, and he's a bit 'antsy'."

"You're not kidding," muttered Danny crossly as he picked himself up and rubbed his bruises and brushed off the mud from his jeans. He peered carefully over the fence.

Deprived of its target, Mr. McVey's bull pawed the ground, butted a fence post half-heartedly and then started eating some grass.

"Hmm, I guess my lance gave you a shock," muttered Danny ruefully, "but not as big a shock as the one you gave me." The bull cocked his head, looked restless and started pawing the ground again.

"And now I've got to go and find the darn thing." Danny shook his fist at the bull from the safety of the fence. "If you've stepped on it I'll personally escort you to the meat packers." The bull snorted then dropped its head to look for another good clump of grass.

Danny observed the bull carefully. He didn't mind cattle. His Dad used to have a bull, a fat old bull called Angus who was too lazy to run, but this young one was far more lively. Danny walked slowly along his side of the fence to see what the bull would do.

The bull's head shot up... WHACK! It slammed into the fence post beside him. "Drat," said Danny. "I'm going to have to think of something to keep you occupied."

Danny watched the bull for a little longer until it lost interest in him and started to graze again. "OK, so you're into food," said Danny and he carefully backed away from the fence, ran to the barn, and filled a large pail with oats. As he returned to the pasture the bull watched him, shaking its head from side to side, but it had calmed down enough to allow Danny to climb up the fence and dump the oats out on the other side. Suspiciously it lowered its head and approached the pile of oats, snuffled, sneezed, then started to eat.

Slowly and carefully Danny lowered himself from the fence and quietly walked around the outside of the pasture. The bull, intent on its treat, ignored him. Danny ran silently and swiftly until he was level with the dogwood bushes. He glanced back to check the bull was still occupied, then heart in his mouth, slipped over the fence and stealthily crept across the pasture to retrieve his lance and atlatl.

It didn't take long to find the lance. It was lying by the bushes in full view. Relieved, Danny picked it up and checked down the pasture again. The bushes were now between him and the bull, so they gave him a temporary feeling of safety. He peered through them to look for his atlatl.

The light was fading and it was hard to see just where he'd been standing. It was no good, he was going to have to step out in full view.

The bull had stopped feeding but was standing harmlessly by the fence, not looking his way, so Danny carefully stepped around the bushes and tiptoed into the middle of the field. The bull turned its head. Danny froze, hoping the bull would think he was a tree. While he stood there his eyes frantically raked the ground. Where was the atlatl?

The bull dropped its head to eat again and Danny's breath whooshed out in relief. Simultaneously he saw a gleaming in the grass, ran forward and scooped up the atlatl.

That did it. The bull turn around and started up the pasture at a fast trot.

"Oh no, not again," gasped Danny as he sprinted for the fence. "This will kill me."

A low black shape suddenly streaked past him and, barking loudly, headed towards the bull and danced around its heels, distracting it. Danny leaped nimbly over the fence.

"Good boy Ringo," gasped Danny as he reached safety. "Come on, let's leave the silly old beast. Time to go in, you've just earned yourself a dog biscuit."

Boy and dog ran to the house but before Danny closed the kitchen door, he looked back at the pasture.

"You know Ringo, "said Danny thoughtfully. "Those First Nations Hunters must have been the bravest people on earth. Buffalo are a heck of a lot bigger and faster than that bull!"

Chapter Twenty

"Danny, Danny!" Marylise came running across the playing field shouting at the top of her voice. "You're wanted in the office."

"What's up?" asked Danny anxiously as he passed her.

Marylise shrugged. "Dunno, Mr. Hubner just said to give you the message. But he didn't look mad," she added.

Danny heaved a sigh of relief and headed for the school office.

"They're not here, they're meeting in the sick room," said the secretary waving him down the corridor. "You're to wait outside till they're ready."

Apprehensively, Danny headed for the sick room. "I hope it's just that Carol's here," he muttered to himself.

The door was closed, but Danny could hear a hum of voices inside. "Good. It is Carol." Relief washed over him as he recognized her voice, but it was short-lived. His heart gave a lurch when he realized Mr. Berg was also inside... and he sounded angry.

Danny looked up and down the corridor. It was empty, so he hesitantly crept close to the door and listened.

"I'm afraid I cannot agree to that," Mr. Berg was saying. "If I allow one student to get out of doing the report,

119

why shouldn't the other students ask for the same privilege?"

Carol's voice was much quieter, but her clear tones still carried well.

"I am not asking for Danny to be excused doing the report, Mr. Berg. I am asking for him to be allowed to present his work in a different manner. By insisting that Danny present his report in written form you are allowing him only to show how badly he can write and spell. You are not giving him a chance to share his knowledge of the subject he's chosen. What are you testing the students on Mr. Berg... in-depth knowledge of the subject they have researched, or writing and spelling skills?"

"Ms. Wakefield," said Mr. Berg grimly, "spelling and writing skills are an integral part of education."

"Of course," agreed Carol. "But Danny is a student who has a learning disability in that area. Are we going to prevent him shining in other areas because we insist on him presenting information only in the ways he finds difficult?"

"So you think Danny's pretty bright?"

Danny strained but couldn't hear Carol's answer.

There was a pause.

"Look Ms. Wakefield, I'm not sure how much Danny's going to be able to do even if I let him attack his project a different way. Between you and me I think some of the learning disability stuff is a cop out. But I'm willing to give the kid a chance. He's had a tough year and a bit of a break might help his confidence and self-esteem. Let me just figure something out for a second."

In the silence Danny heard a faint rustle of paper then the rumble of Mr. Berg's voice again.

"I have set up the project marks in 5 groups: 20% for presentation, 20% for content, 20% for research, 20% for organization of the information, and 20% for writing and spelling."

Danny could hear the smile in Carol's voice. It was a nice smile. "So if Danny doesn't present a written report, he could still get 80% of his marks?"

"I suppose so," agreed Mr. Berg gruffly. "But what makes you think that Danny Budzynski would get anything like that?"

"Because," Carol's voice was softer now, "all he needs is a chance to prove to you just how bright he is."

Shaken, Danny moved away from the door, leaned his back against the cold concrete wall, and slipped down till he was sitting on the floor. He didn't know whether to laugh or cry. "Mom always said eavesdroppers hear no good of themselves," he thought. "But I can't figure out if what I heard is good or bad. Am I dumb or not?" Danny stuck his head in his hands and waited for his brain to stop whirling.

The voices in the sick room rose and fell for some time, then suddenly the door opened and Mr. Berg strode out. Danny shrank into the wall, relieved when his teacher marched the opposite way without noticing him.

Light footsteps came to the doorway and Carol looked up and down the corridor. Her face brightened. "Ah. There you are, Danny. What are you doing on the floor?"

Sheepishly Danny scrambled to his feet. "Just waiting," he mumbled.

Carol stood aside while Danny entered the sick room, then she carefully closed the door, came over and looked searchingly at his tense face.

"What's the matter, Danny?"

Danny dropped his eyes.

"Danny Budzynski, have you been listening at doors?" Carol wagged her finger in mock anger then came over to him, put her arm around him and hugged hard. "So now you're all mixed up and don't understand anything?"

Danny swallowed hard and nodded.

"Well sit down, and I'll try and explain." Carol ignored the chairs and led Danny over to the bed where they could sit side by side.

"Are you worried?"

Danny gulped. "Kind of. Mr. Berg sounded mad."

"He wasn't really. He was just annoyed with me because I challenged him to rethink his teaching approaches." Carol gave Danny another squeeze. "Besides, Mr. Berg is fair and he never stays angry for long."

"He thinks I'm dumb though. He doesn't believe I can do things," Danny muttered dully.

"Mr. Berg's a good teacher, Danny. He'll give you a chance, then it will be up to you to make the best use of it. OK?"

"OK."

"So... do you want to know about your brain? It's pretty neat!"

"I guess so," said Danny unenthusiastically.

"You've got a good brain, Danny. The tests show that not only are you very bright, but you have what is probably one of the best brains in the class." Carol grinned. "Surprised?"

Danny looked thunderstruck. "As good as Marylise?"

"Maybe even better," said Carol firmly.

"Then how come I'm so stupid?"

"You're not stupid, it's those glitches. The glitches affect your writing and spelling, and your ability with numbers. If you didn't have to write things down you would pass nearly all your tests with top marks because you understand most of the information."

Danny thought carefully. "That makes sense," he agreed. "I know things and I know what words I want to use. They just don't come out right."

"Everyone learns in different ways," Carol continued. "You learn mainly through seeing, touching, and experiencing, not from reading and writing. You find school difficult, because you are being asked to write down what you've learned. Because you can't do that, there is nothing for teachers to mark so they can't figure out how much you know."

Danny nodded sadly. "So I'll always be bottom of the class."

"No," said Carol. "This is the exciting part. We'll find some ways for you to work using your best skills. What are you best at... the thing you do most of without any effort?"

"Talking," said Danny cheekily.

"Right," laughed Carol. "So we are going to start by letting you present your report not in written form, but by talking."

For once Danny was speechless.

"There are going to be some big changes in your life Danny, and they will help you immensely." Carol patted his knee. "Are you having trouble absorbing all this at once?"

"I... I guess so.... It's kind of hard to think straight." Danny stammered.

"That's shock. Don't worry about it. Just hang onto the fact you're really bright and we are going to find some ways around your brain glitches."

Danny nodded.

Carol leaned over the side of the bed, pulled up a paper carrier bag, and took out two small boxes. "Here. These are to help you with your work."

Danny took the smallest one first and opened it. "A CALCULATOR!" he yelled. "A calculator! Hey, now I can do my times tables." Danny pressed buttons frantically. "What's 9 times 7, Carol... Do you know?"

Carol laughed and shook her head.

"It's 63!" Danny turned the calculator around so she could see the answer. "Let's try a hard one... What's 1897 times..."—Danny thought for a minute—"er.... 42?"

Carol threw up her hands in horror.

"See... it can do it. It says 79,674!" Danny jumped off the bed in excitement and walked around the room while pressing the magical buttons and watching wonderful combinations of numbers compute before his eyes. Then he closed the calculator with a snap and hugged it close to his chest. "What about Mr. Berg?" he asked Carol. "Will he take this off me?"

"No," said Carol decisively. "But he'll tell you when you can use it. You won't be able to use it all the time, Danny.

It's important for you to learn the methods of doing math, then when you understand what you are doing, you will be able to use the calculator to get the correct answer and to help with your homework."

Danny gave a sigh of relief. "Does it belong to the school?" he asked tentatively, "or is it mine?" he finished hopefully.

"It's yours. Your parents have paid for it, but I chose it to be sure we got the right one for your needs."

Danny lovingly placed the calculator in his pocket and looked over at the other parcel. "And that's mine too?"

Carol smilingly handed it to him.

Danny eagerly lifted the lid of the box. "HEY! a cassette tape recorder... and tapes!" He looked wickedly across at Carol. "Are these the Barenaked Ladies?"

"They're blank at the moment, but they are going to be your stories."

"They are?" Danny looked baffled and turned the tapes over and over in his hands. "I don't get it."

"The tape recorder will help in several ways Danny, but first in language classes. Normally when you're asked to make up a story, you have trouble writing it down, don't you?"

"Yeah... I only get one line done so, no one ever gets to know what my stories are about," said Danny sadly. "And I've thought up some great stories."

"Exactly." Carol tapped the tape recorder. "So now you get to make up your story by speaking into the tape, telling it first. That way your teacher can listen to the story and mark it on content and the way you've organized your thoughts, then we'll get you some help to write it down."

Danny's eyes widened. "Someone will help me write?"

"Sure. The stories will still be your ideas and words, but a teacher's aide or your mom or dad will help you with the spelling."

Danny hopped around the room excitedly. "Hey, I have this terrific story about a giant grasshopper that eats people. It's a mutant caused by an atom explosion way out in the Pacific Ocean and there's only one person who knows how to alter the grasshopper's DNA molecules and kill it."

"Enough, enough." Carol waved her hands in the air. "Get it down on the tape tonight, Danny. It sounds terrific, but I'm running out of time."

"OK... I'll shut up." Danny plonked himself down on the bed again and grinned at her. "This is like Christmas. What else is there?"

"Greedy." Carol ruffled his hair. "There's nothing else, but there might be later on..." she paused teasingly.

"Well, go on... what is it... come on Carol, tell me?" Danny pleaded.

"If all this goes well, we might be able to arrange time for you on a computer in the months ahead."

"Fantastic." Then Danny calmed down a little. "But how is a computer going to help me in school?"

"It will help you with your writing and spelling Danny. It won't happen overnight, but by learning to use the word processing program on a computer you will be able to write more and to correct your own mistakes. This will help what we call the 'patterning' of your brain. Gradually, the more you write on the computer, your spelling will improve."

Carol paused and looked seriously at Danny. "You are very lucky, Danny. Not every child with learning disabilities has parents and a school prepared to help them with the tools they need. Look after them."

"I will, I will," said Danny fervently.

"In the meantime your mom will bring you into Calgary every Saturday so you and I can work together on patterning your brain with numbers and letters."

Danny shook his head to clear it. "Wow, my brain's mush. I can't take in any more."

"I'm not surprised." Carol stood up and stretched. "I'm feeling pretty mushy myself. Off you go to class. Discuss this tonight with your folks. Mr. Berg will talk to you about the report presentation and I'll see you next Saturday."

"Thanks Carol." Danny hesitated at the door then flung himself across the room, hugged her, and ran.

Chapter Twenty-One

The gentle revolution in Danny's life continued slowly and surely, though he still hated math and continued to struggle at the bottom of that subject.

"Check the answer on your calculator," became Mr. Berg's constant refrain.

"I did," cried Danny in frustration, "but my stupid brain made me punch the numbers in the wrong way 'round."

"Michael. Watch Danny enters the numbers in the right order," suggested Mr. Berg. So slowly and with help, Danny would try again.

The language arts classes were totally different.

"Can we hear one of Danny's stories," came the request a number of times when Mr. Berg asked the class for suggestions for a 10 minute filler at the end of the day.

The tape of the Giant Mutant Grasshopper had proved an instant success. Danny experimented and made it into a four-part serial with sound effects. Brett Gibson became so hooked he allowed his helicopter to be borrowed to make authentic sounds for the episode featuring kamikaze pilots trying to shoot down the giant grasshopper as it flew over the Rockies. In the grand finale, Danny gleefully described the laser death ray that finally zapped the giant as it flew over Lake Louise. The ray turned the grasshopper to green slime that slowly dripped through the air and trailed over the lake, the final blob landing SPLAT on a tour bus.

"And that is why Lake Louise is so green," finished Danny's voice with a flourish.

Mr. Berg laughed so hard tears came to his eyes. Especially when he discovered the oozy green slime sounds were made by Danny walking in his dad's rubber boots through a patch of mucky cow pasture.

✿

In between his school work and home activities, Danny worked on his Socials project.

On the day of his presentation to the class, Mr. Budzynski drove Danny to school. Mike was waiting. Carefully he and Danny carried in what looked like four large boxes taped together. Mr. Berg cleared room on his desk and the mysterious package was set down carefully. Mr. Berg wrote out a Do Not Touch sign with (And that means you too, Brett) underneath, and stuck it on the top of the boxes. Danny ran out to the car and fetched one more box.

"Good luck son, I'll be thinking of you," shouted his father as he drove off.

"You scared?" asked Mike curiously as he opened the classroom door so Danny could edge through without dropping anything.

"A bit," admitted Danny. "But not as scared as I was when I thought about doing a written report."

Michael rolled his eyes. "You're nuts—rather you than me."

✿

The presentation started after morning recess. The class filed in followed by Mr. Hubner and Danny's mother.

Danny frowned. "I didn't know you were coming," he whispered as she passed.

"Neither did I, but Mr. Hubner invited me this morning," she whispered back. "Do you mind?"

"Guess not... just didn't know you and the principal were going to be here." Danny walked to the front of the class and stood fidgeting by Mr. Berg's desk. He looked quite calm, but his heart was thumping, cold sweat was trickling down his spine and he felt decidedly ill. "Wish I wasn't doing this," he thought miserably. "What if I mess up?"

"Hey... gonna open the box and let the monkey out, Danny?" called Brett Gibson from across the classroom.

"Looks like it's already out," retorted Danny swiftly. The class giggled and Danny's tension eased a little.

Mr. Berg entered, smiled at Danny and spoke to the class.

"For the next few minutes we are going to listen to an experiment. We all know Danny has trouble with writing. But that shouldn't affect his research skills. So, instead of handing in a written Socials project Danny has chosen to present his knowledge to the class as a talk." Mr. Berg placed his hand on Danny's shoulder. "I have no idea what Danny is going to come up with..." he paused and let the tension grow, "but having had a preview of what is in the box, I think you are in for a treat." Mr. Berg gave Danny's shoulder an encouraging squeeze and went to sit at the back beside the principal.

The moment had arrived. Danny stepped forward, opened his mouth to speak, and promptly went into deep freeze mode.

For a long terrible minute Danny fought a terror so strong he could neither move or speak. His brain quit, his mouth dried, his throat clenched, his knees shook and the audience before him dissolved into a vague mass that advanced and receded as he looked at it. His eyes frantically ranged around looking for escape, and if his legs could have moved he would have run from the room.

As he thrust his hands into his pockets to hide their shaking, his scared eyes caught sight of his mother.

She was leaning forward at the back of the room, her eyes on Danny as though willing him to look her way. One hand was patting the top of her chest and as Danny looked her she mouthed, "BREATHE DEEPLY."

Danny took a deep shuddering breath, and at the same time the hand in his pocket found the lance point. Danny clutched it as a life line and slowly brought it out. The room stopped retreating and advancing and the terror subsided.

"I guess this is what started it all," said Danny clearly, and he pulled out the point and held it up so the whole class could see. "It's a lance point I found. It's called a Scottsbluff point and I found it in a field near here. It was made by a First Nations person 8000 years ago."

From that moment on, the class was hooked.

Danny spoke about trying to knap a stone point himself and how difficult it was. He reached in the small box and pulled out the collection of rock shards that he'd made in his den. The class chuckled with him when he held up some of the funny shapes that had resulted.

While Danny reached in the box again, he spoke of trying to imagine the person who had made the real lance point, and he lifted up a large roll of paper and shook it out.

A young hunter with one eagle feather in his head band gazed proudly out of the picture. He was standing in a coulee, the rock shards fallen at his feet. One hand still held the piece of stone he had used to knap with and the other held the finished point up to catch the sun. The light sparkled off the translucent edges.

"Did you draw that?" asked Marylise with awe in her voice. "It's good."

Mr. Berg moved forward. "That's wonderful Danny. Let me clip it to the board so we can see it while you talk."

Pleased, Danny handed the paper to his teacher, and Mr. Berg hung it up.

"I already knew that the stone points were bound onto the end of wooden lances," Danny continued, "so I had a go at making one."

He lifted up his lance with his best homemade spear point bound to the end. He showed it to the class. "What I didn't know," he explained, "was that the First Nations hunters had something to help them throw these lances further. It has a great name..."

Danny rummaged in the box and with a conjurer's flourish brought out his polished grooved and knobbed stick. "It's called an atlatl."

Danny passed the lance and atlatl to the kids sitting on the front row. "You can look at these," he said. "Then we'll go outside afterwards and I'll demonstrate how they work."

There was a buzz of excitement as the students passed around the two objects.

Danny held up his hand for silence and looked seriously at the class.

"But the best thing that happened because I found the Scottsbluff point, was that I got to know a real Peigan. I got to know my friend Joshua."

Danny spoke of his friendship with Joshua and their visit to Head-Smashed-In Buffalo Jump, and he told of his meeting with the old man.

"Joshua calls him 'Naaahsa'. That's Blackfoot for 'Grandfather', but he's not like any grandfather I've met before..." Danny hesitated, searching for the right words. "He's special... He's an Elder and when he talks... he makes me see pictures in my head.... he tells me things in a way I can really understand them... and this is one of the pictures he helped me see..." Danny looked at his teacher and Mr. Berg walked forward to the edge of the desk and together he and Danny carefully lifted the cardboard box top clear.

The class craned forward and 27 voices gasped in admiration.

Danny had crafted a elaborate papier maché model of Head-Smashed-In Buffalo Jump.

"Guess you all know where this is," Danny grinned, and the class nodded and giggled, "because it's just down the road from here. But this is how it works..."

Danny fiddled in his box again and brought out dozens of tiny brown pipe cleaner buffalo. He placed them as a herd on the upper hillside of the model and reached in his box again. This time he brought out the holy woman. He place her at the bottom of the jump and he explained how she 'called' the herd and sang to the iniskim.

The class leaned forward over their desks, eyes wide with fascination.

Next Danny brought out more pipe cleaner people. Some were the runners, hiding in the hills and spying on the herd, a couple were on hands and knees, with tiny wolf skins on their backs.

"It's scary hunting buffalo," said Danny. "They are so big and so fast and I guess most lances would just injure them and make them even more angry. These people would have to be brave and strong and work carefully together or they'd get trampled."

Danny made his model people stalk the buffalo and moved the herd down to the valley funnels running towards the cliff edge. Then, with a yell that made everyone jump out of their seats, Danny pulled a string and cardboard cut-out people hidden behind the rock piles shot up, showing how the buffalo were startled into their fatal stampede.

The class rose to their feet, rushed forward and crowded around the desk.

"Do it again Danny, show us how it worked," begged Brett Gibson.

Danny looked utterly nonplussed. "I... I've not finished, yet. I've got more to say... I haven't shown you all my scrap book yet." He looked to Mr. Berg for help.

Mr. Berg laughed and slapped him on the back. "The price of being too successful Danny... Didn't you realize how long you spoke to us all?"

Danny shook his head. "No."

"It's nearly lunch time! There's just time for you to show the class how the model works and we'll have to dismiss. We'll look at your scrap book this afternoon, and maybe you could demonstrate the atlatl."

"Isn't it a great model, Mr. Berg?" Mike jumped up and down excitedly. "Wasn't that a great report? How many marks are you going to give Danny? Should be good, eh?"

Danny stiffened.

The class stopped what they were doing and turned to Mr. Berg.

"Hmmm." Mr. Berg spoke slowly and thoughtfully, "I marked all the rest of you using the five areas we discussed in class. Now let's see... presentation was the first one," he grinned. "I guess we can't fault Danny on that one. He did a different kind of presentation from the rest of you but he spoke like a professional and used pictures and objects. Your talk was really well rehearsed Danny."

Danny and his mother grinned at each other.

"Should get full marks for that," said a voice from the back. Several class members nodded in agreement.

"Now, content," Mr. Berg paused. "You know Danny, I have to give you full marks both for content and for research. In fact..." he looked around thoughtfully, "I think you did more actual research that anyone else in the class."

"He sure did," agreed Mike, "with the trip to Head-Smashed-In, and the museum here and stuff, as well as all the books he read."

"Your organization of facts was excellent too," continued Mr. Berg. "You went smoothly from one topic to the other and didn't miss things out." He paused. "Unfortunately one of the areas I also marked was for writing and spelling. Now Danny hasn't done a written report so I guess I can't give him the 20% in that area."

Danny looked down and shuffled his feet.

"Hey!... That's not fair," said Marylise. "Danny had to talk to the whole class," she looked around at the back of the class, "even the principal," she pointed out.

"Yeah. That's harder than writing," said someone else. "I'd die."

"Danny did some stuff no-one else did," pointed out Michael. "That model's far out."

Everyone looked accusingly at Mr. Berg.

"You think I need to mark Danny's finished project a different way then?" Mr. Berg asked.

Everyone nodded.

"OK. I think Danny deserves.... 99%."

The class clapped and cheered and crowded around Danny.

"Hey, how does it feel to be top of the class for once?" laughed Michael.

At first Danny couldn't answer. "99 per cent?" he whispered unbelievingly. "99 per cent?" Then he looked up at his teacher questioningly.

"What did I lose the one percent on Mr. Berg? What did I fail at?"

With a big grin Mr. Berg whipped a large black felt tip pen out of his pocket and handed it to Danny. "You handed in your work without your name on it Danny," he laughed.

And they all watched while Danny, hands shaking, scrawled his signature on the base of the model.

Chapter Twenty-Two

The board meeting in the museum was in full progress. Seventeen men and women sat silently around a large polished table.

Eventually the chairperson stirred. "It's tricky alright, Charlie," she said. "If we don't handle this right and the Peigans decide to make a fuss, it could hit national news."

"Right, that's all we need, a confrontation," muttered a voice from the far end of the table.

Charlie Budzynski shook his head. "No, no, don't exaggerate. That's not an issue. This request hasn't come officially from the Peigan people. It's just something my son found out and felt strongly enough about to want me to point out to the board. Mind you..." he added thoughtfully, "if we handle it right, it could do us a lot of good."

"Well, I think it's ridiculous," said Mrs. Saunders forthrightly. "Why should a 10-year-old boy dictate to us what photos we can hang in our museum? Photos don't hurt anyone."

"Nobody's 'dictating', Mrs. Saunders." Mr. Berg leaned forward and looked across at the chairperson. "Danny's in my class, and it was through a Socials project he researched that he came across this information. He's a bright boy, I was most impressed with his project and the accuracy of his research. I think we should give him and his friend a hearing, then decide what to do."

The rest of the board nodded in agreement, so the chairperson went to the door and ushered in a scared-looking Danny and Joshua.

The chairperson smiled at them and pulled forward two seats. "Thank you for coming to our meeting, please sit down."

Danny and Joshua perched uneasily on the edge of their chairs while the chairperson turned to the board members. "This is Danny Budzynski and his friend, Joshua Brokenhorn."

Everyone looked at them.

"Come on Danny," whispered Joshua nudging him in the ribs. "Say your bit and let's get out of here."

Danny gulped. This was far worse than the class project. He looked around wildly and saw his father and Mr. Berg sitting together. They both smiled encouragingly.

"It's about the display in the museum, in the First Nations gallery." His voice came out tight and high in the big room. Danny cleared his throat and started again.

"See... I've been to the museum a lot for a couple of years... And... and the thing I liked best was the photograph of the Sundance."

Everyone nodded understandingly.

"But then I got to know Joshua here and... and I did some research and listened to Joshua and his grandfather... and I found out that the photo shouldn't be here at all." He finished in hurry.

"That photo was given to us by the Glenbow Museum in Calgary. What is good enough for them is surely good enough for us," said Mrs. Saunders flatly.

"But the people at the Glenbow museum aren't Peigan," said Danny earnestly. "To First Nations people the Sundance is sacred. It should never have been photographed as it's too holy. The ceremonies are kept secret and it's a ceremony that they don't choose to share with white people."

"Is this true?" said one of the other board members to Joshua.

Joshua spoke in a voice so soft the board had to strain to hear him. "My grandfather is one of the Peigan elders. He gave Danny the information but he said it's hard for white people to understand."

"So what do they want us to do with the photo?" asked another member of the board.

Danny shrugged. "I dunno. I never asked. In fact the elders never asked me to come here... It was just my idea." he finished miserably. "I just didn't feel good seeing the photo any more when I knew it was wrong. I think the elders would like it taken down." Joshua nodded in agreement.

"Thank you Joshua, Danny. We really appreciate you giving us this information. The board will discuss the issue and let you know." The chairperson rose and opened the door for them. Danny and Joshua filed out and the door closed behind them.

"What now?" Joshua asked, as he and Danny walked moodily down the sidewalk. "Do you think they'll take the picture down?"

Danny shrugged.

Joshua sighed philosophically. "Well, we tried. See you tomorrow morning?"

"I can't." Danny looked uncomfortable. "There's something I've got to do."

"I'm working for your Dad in the afternoon."

Danny grinned. "Want me to come and scoop? I'll teach you how to do a quad."

"Only if you promise not to touch the till." Joshua fled, laughing, with Danny in full pursuit.

✿

The next morning Danny had set his alarm early. There was only a hint of daylight as he quietly dressed and tiptoed out of the house. He headed west across the fields jogging through the farm lands until he came to the prairie bluffs on the banks of the Oldman River.

The sunrise was liquid gold. It spilled across the sky, firing the tips of the distant mountains then flooded down across the prairie, gilding every blade of grass.

Danny moved slowly across the bluffs, eyes down, searching. He was looking for something he'd found on a postcard and pasted in his scrapbook, something Joshua had said could be seen on these bluffs. An inconspicuous tipi circle. Slowly and carefully his eyes raked the ground.

There, he found it, a stone half hidden in the grass, and another, and another. A half-buried circle of stones, all that remained of a long-gone tipi encampment on the banks of the Oldman River.

Danny stepped gently into the centre of the stone circle and stood, alone with his thoughts. He then put his hand in his pocket, slowly pulled out the Scottsbluff point and held it up to the sunrise.

It glowed.

"You helped me, but you don't belong to me," Danny whispered. "But I can't bear to give you to a museum. You belong here, on the prairie, with the spirits of the people who made you." He knelt down, gathered a handful of fragrant sage and wrapped it around the point.

Carefully placing the package on the ground, Danny moved to the edge of the tipi ring and loosened one of the stones. Gently he lifted it out, placed it on the grass, and scratched a hollow in the soft earth where the stone had been. He returned purposefully to the circle centre. Very gently he picked up the fragrant package with one hand and reached into his pocket with the other. He pulled out a willow whistle.

Holding the package before him, Danny blew to the north, the south, the east, and the west, summoning the newly-awakened world to witness his actions, then returned to the hollow.

Tenderly he fitted the package into the earthy nest, replaced the stone and adjusted the surrounding moss and lichen to fit. He blew on the top and the leftover dust scattered. There was nothing to show what he had done.

Danny moved back into the centre of the circle and picked another handful of sage. He crumbled it in his hands, breathing in the heady scent, then he lifted his hands in the air. "I give you back to the earth," he whispered, "but one day, let someone else like me borrow you for a while." He spread his fingers and watched the sage dust disperse on the breath of the early morning breeze.

Above him, a black silhouette circled majestically as a bald eagle soared overhead. Danny squinted up with eyes half shut against the brightness as it circled nearer the sun.

As he watched, a small black dot seemed to detach before the eagle disappeared. Danny's body became at one with the earth. Only his eyes moved, following the black speck as it wafted downwards in slow circles. He held his breath, then expelled it in a great sigh as the eagle feather drifted slowly to his feet.

Glossary

Several names or phrases—aboriginal people, First Nations, First People, Indian, and Native—are currently in use to describe Canada's original inhabitants. Some names are more acceptable than others to the people themselves, who often prefer aboriginal people or First Nations. The name "Indian" is still in use in the Federal Indian Act and the names of some established organizations. Characters in the story use the names most appropriate to their background and knowledge at the time they are speaking.

Aboriginal—original inhabitant.
Anthropologist—a person who studies the origins, development and behaviour of people.
Archaeologist—a person who excavates and studies the buried remains of human activity.
Arrowhead—a piece of stone, bone or other material shaped to a point and attached to the head of an arrow.
Atlatl—a short stick with a handle at one end and a hook at the other. It can be used to increase the power and distance with which a lance can be thrown, by extending the natural reach of the thrower's arm.

Bannock—an unleavened bread (made without yeast or other rising agent) originating in Europe but widely used by First Nations.
Beadwork—decorative patterns created by sewing colored beads to clothing, moccasins etc.
Blood—(or *Kainaawa*) One of three nations belonging to the Blackfoot Confederacy, now with a reserve north of Cardston, Alberta.
Blackfoot—(or *Siksikawa*) One of three nations belonging to the Blackfoot Confederacy, now with a reserve near Gleichen, Alberta.
Blackfoot Confederacy—a group of First Nations most recently living in what is now Southern Alberta and Northern Mon-

tana, comprising the Blackfoot, Blood, and Peigan. All speak the Blackfoot language.

Breech cloth—a cloth worn below the waist.

Buckskin—tanned leather from deer.

Buffalo Jump—a place used in ancient times to catch buffalo, by driving them across level ground and stampeding them over the edge of a cliff.

Chert—a flint-like mineral which flakes leaving sharp edges, and was often used before metals were available for making arrowheads and other tools.

Confederacy—a group of people joined together.

Coulee—a dry valley in the prairies.

Cree Nation—a group of First Peoples most recently living in the central and eastern prairies and adjacent forests.

Donor—people who give things to museums are called donors. The museum keeps records of the sources of its collections.

First Nations/First People—The original people of North America before European settlement. Many different nations occupied different areas of what is now Canada and the United States.

Flint—a hard mineral which makes a spark against metal, and was used for making fire, for tools in prehistoric times, and for the flints of flintlock guns into the last century.

Flint knapping—the art of shaping flint into tools, by striking raw flint with another stone or metal tool.

Grass dance—a dance of prairie First Nations, in which groups of people dance in a circle, frequently performed at pow wows.

Indian—term once commonly used for First Nations. It reflects the error made by Columbus, who thought he had arrived in India when he reached islands off North America. Although still used, it is generally being replaced by the more accurate terms Aboriginal, First Nations or First People.

Iniskim—a small buffalo-shaped stone, formerly used by First Nations in ceremonies associated with buffalo jumps.

Interpretive Centre—a building with an exhibit designed to tell the story of a site or region.

Irrigation ditch—a ditch dug to carry water for irrigation from a river or lake to dry fields.

Lance point—a point like a large arrowhead, made to be attached to a lance, or throwing spear.

Learning Disability—a mental dysfunction distinct from intelligence which makes it difficult for someone to learn.

L.D.—a common abbreviation for Learning Disability.

Moccasin—a shoe made of leather, originally by First Nations people. Moccasins are often decorated with beadwork.

Naaahsa—Blackfoot name for grandfather.

Native—original inhabitant.

North West Mounted Police—the original police force created in 1873 and sent to the prairies by the Government of Canada.

Oldman River—a river running through southern Alberta, named after the Old Man, a divine trickster of the Blackfoot religion.

Palisade—a barrier made of upright tree trunks set in the ground.

Peigan—one of the three nations belonging to the Blackfoot Confederacy, now with a reserve near Brocket, west of Fort Macleod, Alberta.

Perogy, perogies—a dumpling containing a meat, cheese or vegetable filling, associated in Canada with people of Ukrainian descent.

Pow Wow—a First Nations gathering, which may include religious, ceremonial and social aspects.

Prairie—level or rolling land largely covered with grass and sometimes sage.

Reserve—short for Indian Reserve. A piece of land set aside by the government, usually by treaty, for the exclusive use of one or more groups of First Peoples.

Runs—an area marked off by piles of stones, through which buffalo were stampeded to a buffalo jump.

Scottsbluff point—a lance point of a particular kind, used around 8500 years ago.

Sinew—a tough tissue that connects bones and muscles. Sinew from bison and deer was often used for attaching lance points to lances.

Slough (pronounced *sloo*)—a low area in the prairies full of water in wet periods, but often drying out in summer.

Stetson—a wide-brimmed hat commonly worn on the prairies.

Stockade—a palisaded enclosure. A stockade known as a pound was often used to catch buffalo where no cliffs were available.

Sweetgrass—a grass used ceremonially by First Nations. It is collected by elders, dried, and burnt as incense on ceremonial occasions.

Tipi—a collapsible tent made originally of buffalo hides, supported on a conical framework of tree trunks. The covers were traditionally painted with designs of great significance to the owners.

Tipi rings—a ring of stones once used to hold down the edges of a tipi. When the tipi is removed, these are left on the prairie, and if undisturbed, show the former presence of traditional camping places.

Acknowledgements

This book would not have been possible without help from the following people and organizations: Alberta Foundation for the Literary Arts, Canada Council, Alberta Culture, Alberta Historic Sites, Bob Kidd at the Provincial Museum of Alberta, Chris Williams, Kenneth Eagle Speaker, Wilford the storyteller, Joe Crowshoe and other members of the staff and volunteers at Head-Smashed-In Buffalo Jump, Fort Macleod Museum, Lethbridge Community College, Eldon Yellowhorn, David and Ian Rowe, Rika Ruebsaat and Karen Kovach from Learning Disabled Student Services at the University of Alberta. Special acknowledgement to Guy Chadsey and Antonia Banyard at Beach Holme for their enthusiastic support.

A very special thanks is due to David and Lucy Spalding who untiringly read, re-read and commented on the many drafts. Without Dave's untiring correction of my garbled spelling that baffles spell checkers, this book would not have happened. David also prepared the glossary.